candy apple books . . .
just for you.
sweet. fresh. fun.
take a bite!

ACCIDENTALLY Fabulous

by Lisa Papademetriou

SCHOLASTIC INC.

New York Toronto London Auckland Sydney
Mexico City New Delhi Hong Kong Buenos Aires

To Catherine Daly,
the most fabulous girl I know

ISBN-13: 978-0-545-04667-1
ISBN-10: 0-545-04667-X

12 11 10 9 8 7 6 5   11 12 13/0
Printed in the U.S.A.
First printing, August 2008

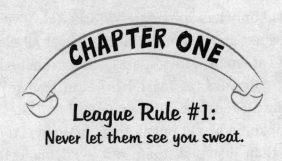

CHAPTER ONE

League Rule #1:
Never let them see you sweat.

"What do you call that outfit?" My older brother, Kirk, looked me over and smirked as he pulled a carrot stick from a silver platter. "'Amy Flowers Wears Waitress Chic'?"

"What do you call *that* outfit?" I shot back, pointing at his chest. "'I've Only Got One Tie'?"

Kirk grimaced at his tie, which featured neon-colored cartoon fish with oversized kissy lips. "This *is* my only tie. Dad made me wear it." He swiped his shaggy brown hair out of his eyes, but it fell right back into place. I'm surprised he doesn't go around bumping into walls all day.

"You could have borrowed one of Dad's ties," I pointed out.

"Dad only has *striped* ties," Kirk said. "I've only got striped shirts. I'm not about to get all clashy-clashy at some fancy party." He crunched his carrot. "Besides, at least I have an excuse. You actually picked that outfit yourself."

I looked down at my clothes. Actually, I'd done more than just pick them out — I'd made them. Well, I'd made the black satin skirt. The tuxedo shirt was something I'd found at a local thrift store called Retread. I'd cut off the sleeves and taken in the waist so that it was fitted and tucked neatly into the skirt's wide band. And I'd found this amazing black flower-print bag to go with it. It was oversized and had long handles that fit over my shoulder — it was perfect to carry all of my stuff. "Do I really look like a waitress?" I asked, suddenly wishing that I hadn't decided to get creative with my clothes for Uncle Steve's engagement party.

Kirk shrugged, reaching for a broccoli spear. "Not really," he admitted. "I just like to torture you. Hey, you want anything? I'm going to get some punch."

"I'm good." I watched him blend into the crowd that milled around the ballroom. Kirk hadn't been kidding — this really was a fancy party. Mom had warned me that Uncle Steve's fiancée was seriously into style and even owned one of the coolest boutiques in town, Bounce. Still. Somehow, I hadn't been prepared for this party — its Arabian Nights theme, complete with giant brass candelabras, plush red fabric draped along the walls, and even a belly dancer in a purple outfit with gold chains at her waist. I had lost sight of my parents long ago — they had disappeared among the swirl of elegantly dressed guests. Which was pretty amazing, given that my parents are not exactly Mr. and Mrs. Elegant. In fact, this was the first time I'd seen my mother in a skirt since Easter three years ago. And my dad — his idea of a fashion statement is a sweater vest.

"How's my favorite Amy?" boomed a voice behind me.

"Uncle Steve!" He was standing with a very pretty girl who looked about my age. She had blond hair that gleamed past her shoulders, and she was wearing a gorgeous turquoise dress with crystals at the neckline and hem. Uncle Steve was wearing a tuxedo — white tie. I've always thought that he looks a bit like Frosty the Snowman — he's heavyset with a round face and a shiny bald head. And he's almost always cheerful and smiling, like he was right then. "Here's someone I thought you should meet!"

"Jenelle?" I asked. I was pretty sure that I recognized her from the photo Uncle Steve had showed me a couple of weeks ago. Only the girl in the photo had been smiling — a huge, wide smile. She'd been standing on the beach with her mother, both wearing floppy straw hats and big grins.

But the girl in front of me wasn't smiling. She shifted her weight from one foot to the other, uncomfortably. "Hi," she said.

"You two are going to the same school in the fall," Uncle Steve announced. "Jenelle, I've already told Amy all about you!"

"I've been dying to meet you," I told Jenelle, which was true. It was going to be my first year at Allington Academy, and I didn't know anyone there. I'd spent sixth grade at Langton Middle School. I was in the magnet program and loved it. But when Dad got a summer job teaching at Allington, he managed to get me an interview with the admissions director. Allington Academy is a private school here in Houston, probably the best in the state. When I saw the high-tech science labs, the incredibly huge auditorium, the black box performance area, the super-green grounds, the documentary screening room, the laptops that

4

were provided for every student, and the library — the ginormous library — well, when I saw all of that, I fell instantly in love. I knew I *had* to go there. Still, I didn't think it was possible. Allington is the fanciest school in Houston . . . and the most expensive. But then the admissions people offered me a full scholarship.

Cue the "happy ending" music.

"Aren't you so excited for school to begin?" I said to Jenelle. "I mean, I love summer, too, but I never mind going back to school."

Jenelle gave me a distracted smile. "I can wait," she admitted.

"Uncle Steve said that you're in seventh grade, too."

Jenelle cocked her head. "So, are we going to be, like, cousins?" she asked.

I laughed. "Uncle Steve isn't really my uncle. He and my dad are best friends, not brothers."

A waiter in a white shirt and black pants stopped in front of Jenelle and held out a silver tray loaded with tiny crab cakes. "Thanks," I said, taking one. Jenelle shook her head at the waiter as I popped the warm, spicy hors d'oeuvre into my mouth. "Don't you want one?" I asked her. "They're delicious."

She smiled weakly. "I'm too nervous."

"About what?" I asked, hiking my bag higher onto my shoulder.

Jenelle lifted her delicate eyebrows at me. "Ever been to your own mother's engagement party?" she asked.

I winced. "Good point."

Jenelle sighed, scanning the crowd. "My dad's here, too, with his new girlfriend," she said. She shook her head and a lock of perfect blond hair fell behind her shoulder. "This whole thing is so bizarre."

"Well, I guess it's good that your parents still get along," I said. "I have a friend whose parents haven't spoken in ten years."

"Yeah." Jenelle smiled at me, but it was a sort of sad smile. "I guess."

Comfortable silence settled between us, and the band started to play some dance music. Not very Arabian Nights, but I guess not everyone's down with the whole belly-dancing thing.

"Hey, do you want to head out to the patio?" I asked. "It's a little warm in here."

"Yeah, and it sounds like the band's playing songs from the eighties." Jenelle rolled her eyes. "That means my mom will start dancing soon."

I grinned. "Mine, too. Let's escape while we can."

She flashed me a grateful smile and I led the way toward the French doors that opened onto the brick patio. It was lush with pretty tropical plants and pink bougainvillea dripping down the walls. Hurricane lamps with candles lined a low brick planter that circled the space, and there were café tables and chairs for people who wanted a quieter spot to chat. The place was empty.

There were two steps that led down onto the patio. They were kind of hard to see, and I was just about to say, "Watch out for these steps," when Jenelle let out a little cry and stumbled against me. I heard a small rip, and Jenelle's hazel eyes went round in horror. "What happened?" I asked.

"My heel," she said, fumbling with her hem. "It got caught." Sure enough, part of her hem was ripped out, creating a ragged line at the edge of her dress.

"It's okay," I said quickly. I could see that Jenelle was fighting back tears.

She shook her head. "My mom is going to *freak*."

"No, it's really okay," I told her. I plunked my huge handbag onto a café table and started rummaging around inside.

Jenelle took off her turquoise mule and scowled

at it. "At least the heel isn't broken," she said. Finally, she seemed to notice my huge handbag. "What have you got in there?"

I shrugged. "Everything."

She eyed my bag doubtfully. "A sewing kit?"

"Almost," I told her, pulling a mini-stapler from my bag.

"Wait." She held up a hand as if she was about to push me away. "What are you —"

"Trust me, I've done this a million times." And before she had a chance to say no, I flipped up the raw edge of her dress, turned it under neatly, and stapled twice. "See?" I said, dropping the hem back into place. "Problem solved."

Jenelle blinked. Then she held up the hem for a better look. "You can't even see the staple," she said.

"The long edge is on the inside," I told her. Four tiny silver slivers were almost invisible among the crystals at the hem.

Jenelle smiled at me — a real smile. And it lit up her whole face. She looked exactly the way she looked in that photo Uncle Steve had showed me. "You're a lifesaver," she said, giving me a quick hug. "I can't believe you stapled my skirt — I never would have thought of it!"

"It's no big deal," I said, blushing a little. Still, it felt good to make Jenelle so happy. *I've just made my first friend at Allington Academy*, I thought.

"Jenelle!"

A girl with long, sleek black hair and the sharpest cheekbones I'd ever seen appeared in the doorway. She had on a deep blue dress and wore a sapphire-and-diamond pendant at her neck. The girl smiled, but it wasn't a smile that made her look pretty. She was holding a plate with a single carrot in one hand and a half-empty glass in the other. "I've been looking all over for you."

"Oh hi, Fiona." Jenelle slipped her mule back onto her right foot.

"When I heard the band, I thought maybe you'd tried to disappear out the back door," Fiona said with a smirk. She drained her glass, then put it on the plate and shoved both in my direction, barely glancing at me. "Would you mind bringing me some more punch?"

"Fiona, this is Amy." Casting me a sideways glance, Jenelle took the plate and placed it on the nearest table. "She's Steve's best friend's daughter."

"What?" Fiona's blue eyes widened. "Omigosh, I'm *so* sorry!" A tight little smile twisted at the corner

9

of her mouth. "It's just — your outfit makes you look like a caterer." She blinked at me innocently.

"I think Amy's outfit is cool," Jenelle said quickly. "I really like the skirt."

"I made it," I told her.

"Oh, you *made* it," Fiona gushed as if she was talking to a three-year-old. "That's so *cute!* You don't have to worry that someone will have seen that outfit in a magazine. And nobody else is wearing the same thing — except the waitstaff." She laughed a little.

It's just a joke, I told myself. *Don't strangle her.*

Jenelle smiled weakly and shook her head. "Fiona, Amy is going to Allington this year."

"Really?" Fiona folded her arms across her chest and gave me an up-and-down look. "That will be *so* interesting for you. Well!" She dug her perfectly manicured nails into Jenelle's arm. "Come on, Jenelle! Let's go see if the band knows any music from this millennium!" And with that, she dragged Jenelle through the French doors and into the bustle of the party.

I hesitated a moment, wondering if I should follow them. I didn't think Jenelle would mind, but Fiona was another story. . . .

"Hey, there you are." Just then, Kirk trotted down the patio steps, holding out his plate.

"Okay, I get it," I snapped. "You already told me — I look like a waitress!"

Kirk frowned. "What's your deal? I just thought you might want one of these cornbread muffin things," he said. "The shrimp is really good, too. But if you don't want it . . ."

I winced. "No — I do. Thanks," I said, taking a mini-muffin from his plate.

"So . . ." Kirk turned to gaze at the crowd. "What do you think of the party?"

"I don't know." I spotted Jenelle and Fiona at the edge of the stage. It looked like Fiona was giving orders to the bandleader. He was nodding furiously, like he was memorizing every word that dropped from her mouth. "I guess I haven't made up my mind yet," I said.

"Omigosh, Blake totally *loves* this band," Elise said, holding up a CD with an orange cover. THE BEAT DETECTIVES, it read over a picture of a man in a black suit with a bright green apple in the place where his head should be. I love the art that bands slap on their CD covers — it never makes any sense. "Do you think I should get it for him?" The stack of silver bangles on her wrist jingled as she tucked a few of her braids behind her ear.

"Well — does he have it already?" I asked her. Elise is one of my best friends, but ever since she started dating Blake Bannersly at the end of last year, she's had a total one-track mind.

"I don't know." Elise pursed her lips. "He may have some of the songs on his iPod. Do you think I should call him and ask?"

I continued flipping through the slim plastic boxes in front of me. "He can always return it."

"Amy, you're brilliant!" Elise smiled at the CD, her green eyes twinkling. She flipped it over and started reading the song titles on the back.

"Is it his birthday, or something?" I asked.

"No, why?"

"Then why are you getting him a present?"

Elise sighed heavily and turned her eyes toward the ceiling. She'd been doing that a lot lately, and I have to admit that I found it kind of annoying. "I'm just getting this CD to show him that I'm *thinking* of him," Elise explained, like it couldn't be more obvious. "When you have a boyfriend, you'll understand."

Grr. That's another thing Elise has told me more than once. It's part of the Blake Bannersly Brain Disease that's starting to rot her mind.

I turned back to the rack, and there it was — the CD I'd been looking for, right under my fingertips. Jackpot! It was an import that I'd been wanting for three weeks. Nobody had it — except, of course, for Crank It, my favorite store. It's a dingy hole-in-the-wall in a strip mall at the edge of my neighborhood. It's been around for about a thousand years — they even still sell vinyl records — and the walls are plastered with vintage posters from concerts that the owner actually went to. The bins are jammed with music by hard-to-find bands, and the speakers are always playing something cool that I've never heard before.

Elise arched a brow at my CD. "The Eclectic Misfits?" she asked. "Who's that?"

"They're from Scotland," I explained. "They're excellent."

"Blake really likes this Scottish band called the Tiny Earthquakes," Elise said.

"Hm," I said, since I didn't really know how to reply. Lately, it seemed like every topic in the world led directly back to Blake.

"So, how was the party?" Elise asked as I flipped through the CD racks.

"It was okay," I told her. I didn't really want to get into the whole Obnoxious Fiona thing.

She leaned against the rack, absently tracing her finger over the CD spines. "Are you ready for school on Monday? I can't believe we had to start last week — I'm so jealous." Elise grinned, fluttering her eyelashes. She has really pretty almond-shaped green eyes that she usually plays up with green eye shadow. It sounds over the top, but it isn't — she uses a pale shade that sparkles against her dark cocoa skin. She's really into makeup and totally knows what she's doing when she puts it on. She's tried to help me about a thousand times, but in the end we always agree that it's better if I just stick to fashion. "Then again, what am I talking about? You love school. I'll bet you've bought all of your notebooks and pens already."

I nibbled my lower lip. "I don't know," I admitted. "I'm a little nervous, I guess. I kind of wish we weren't starting so soon."

"Seriously?" Elise planted her hands on her hips. "You? Nervous?"

It was just that ever since the party, I'd started to wonder whether or not I'd fit in at Allington Academy. Both Fiona and Jenelle were so well-dressed and perfect-looking. . . . They looked like they came from the Planet of Gorgeous People. And here I was, with my long frizzy hair, braces on my lower teeth, and homemade-slash-vintage outfits. I looked like I came from . . . well, from *my* house. "I don't really know anyone at Allington," I said.

"Oh, please." Elise waved her hand like she was shooing away a swarm of annoying gnats. "You'll have a zillion friends in about ten minutes. That's what happened at Langton, right?"

"That's true. . . ." I pressed my lips together, thinking, as we stepped up to the counter to pay for our music. My favorite clerk, Roger, was behind the counter. He looks kind of scary — he has an orange Mohawk and a pierced eyebrow — but he's actually a big marshmallow on the inside.

Roger was explaining the store's policy to a disappointed-looking guy. "I'm sorry, but we don't carry Celine Dion," he said. "It's the owner's policy. He only likes to carry more obscure stuff."

"Is there any place close by where I can get her latest album?" the guy asked. He raked a tan hand through his sandy-blond hair. I couldn't help noticing that he was really cute.

Too bad he has such weird taste in music, I thought. Not that there's anything wrong with Celine Dion — it's just an odd choice for a teenage guy.

"It's my mom's birthday," the cute boy added quickly, almost as if he had overheard my brain wave. "She's a huge fan, and I really need to get her present today." He looked kind of desperate.

15

Roger thought it over for a minute. "How close?"

"Walking distance?" the guy asked. "Or running distance?"

Roger shook his head. "I can't think of any place." He turned to me. "Amy? Do you have any ideas?" This is what I like about Roger — he really does try to be helpful.

"Well, if your mom likes Celine Dion, why don't you get her something by someone else who's got kind of a similar sound? Maybe she'd like to try something new."

The cute guy's big brown eyes were hopeful. He had long, dark lashes and a perfectly straight nose. "Do you have any suggestions? I don't really know much about music."

I thought for a moment. "How about Clementine Figueroa?" I suggested. "Or Madeline Mitchell?"

"Maybe Lenora Frist?" Elise toyed with the end of one of her braids. "She's got a great voice." She wiggled her eyebrows at me and grinned. I could tell that she thought the guy was as cute as I did.

"She's got a great voice, but she's funkier than Celine." I turned back to the cute boy. "Your mom will probably like someone with more of a pop sound. Like maybe . . . Angelina Fry?"

"Angelina Fry — good choice," Roger put in.

The cute boy flashed him a doubtful look, as if he didn't believe that someone with an orange Mohawk could be an expert on Celine Dion soundalikes.

"She's got powerhouse pipes," Roger said defensively. "Get her first album, *Speak No Evil* — I guarantee your mom will love it."

"Really?" The cute guy was asking me.

I felt Elise nudge me from behind. I ignored her, and instead nodded at the boy. "Really." I pointed toward the rear of the store. "Under World Music. Check the Fs."

"You're totally saving me," the cute boy said.

I couldn't help laughing a little. "I get that a lot."

He hurried toward the back of the store. I could feel Elise grinning at me as Roger rang up my CD.

"What are you smiling at?" I asked her.

"Noth-ing," she singsonged. "It's just that you didn't seem to have any trouble talking to that cutie."

"So?"

"So!" Elise threw up her hands as if the whole thing was too obvious for words. "What are you worried about Allington for? Blake says you're the world's easiest person to talk to," Elise said. "You'll make tons of friends, you'll see."

"Blake said that?" I asked, surprised. It was a little weird to think that Blake and Elise had been talking about me. Then again, it was nice to know that he thought I could talk to people. . . .

"Everyone says that!" Elise huffed. She flipped her braids over her shoulder, which made the beads at the ends clack indignantly.

"You *are* pretty easy to talk to," Roger volunteered from behind the cash register. "Fifteen dollars and thirty cents."

I couldn't help smiling at him as I handed over the money. "You think so?"

"Definitely," he and Elise chorused. She paid for her CD and tucked both into my huge bag.

"You'll probably even have a boyfriend by the end of the first month," Elise added in a whisper as we walked out of the store. "That would be so great — then you could go on double dates with me and Blake!"

Laughing, I rolled my eyes. "Something to look forward to," I said.

Elise wrapped an arm around me and squeezed. "It sure is!"

CHAPTER TWO

League Rule #2:
It's nice to feel good, but it's better to look good.

"Amy?" Dad called when he heard me open the door. "Is that you?" He walked into the living room, drying his hands on a kitchen towel. Pizza, my small white dog, trotted in after him.

"What smells so good?" I asked, dropping my huge bag by the front door and pausing to scratch Pizza behind the ears. I kicked off my shoes, and Elise did, too.

"Stir-fry in ginger sauce," Dad said, grinning. He's been on an Asian-cooking kick lately, which is more than fine with me. For the past three weeks, every dinner has been spicy and delicious. "Hi, Elise. Are you staying for dinner?"

Elise's eyes were huge — she thinks my dad is just about the best cook in the known universe. "Definitely!" She pulled out her cell phone and started to dial. "Just let me call my mom."

I gave my dad a look. "See?" I said.

"No cell phone."

I sighed. I knew there was no point in arguing. We've been over this ground so many times, it's practically paved. Still, I couldn't help pointing out that I'm one of the few people left on the planet who doesn't have a cell phone.

Elise held her hand over the mouthpiece. "Mom wants to know if you can drop me off after dinner," she said.

"No problem," Dad told her.

"No problem," Elise repeated into the phone. Then she flipped it closed. "Great!"

"Amy, there's a package for you on the kitchen table," Dad said, turning back to rescue his stir-fry.

"Oh, goody, I love packages!" Elise gushed, hurrying to the kitchen. She slipped into a chair and slapped her hands against the wood table eagerly. "Open it, open it, open it!"

I lifted the large box uncertainly. It was wrapped in brown paper and had my name and address on it. But the return address was unfamiliar. "Who's J. Renwick?"

"Who cares?" Elise said. "Open it!"

"Renwick?" The pan on the oven hissed as Dad poured in a bowlful of bok choy. "That's Linda's last name. Steve's fiancée."

"Oh," I said. *J. Renwick must be Jenelle*, I thought. *But why would she send me a package?*

"Oh my gosh, I can't take this," Elise said, slamming the table. "How can you sit there trying to guess who sent it when there's a *package* that needs *opening*?"

"Okay, okay, jeez." I got a pair of scissors out of the junk drawer and cut open the packing tape. Underneath the brown paper was green wrapping with a yellow geometric pattern. At the lower left corner was an elegant gold seal that read BOUNCE. Jenelle's mom's store.

"It's something really good!" Elise clapped her hands. "I can tell!"

I started pulling off the paper in my usual style, slowly and carefully.

"You're making me crazy," Elise said. Reaching out, she ripped off the paper, exposing a white box.

"Elise!" I said.

She pointed a finger at me. "Just let me do it," she said. "It's a small price to pay for my mental sanity."

I rolled my eyes as Elise pulled off the lid. *It's amazing what someone can get away with when they've been your friend since second grade*, I thought, watching Elise yank aside layers of fluffy purple tissue paper.

"Whoa!" She held up a super-cool crinkly cotton shirt. It was a deep rose-pink and fitted. "And pants!" Elise pulled out a pair of light pink capris. She checked the label and gasped. "They're Annabelle Jacobsen! Oh wow. Oh wow. I feel a little dizzy. Can I get a glass of water?" Elise put her hands to her temples and swayed slightly, as if she had just won the lottery. She can be a little bit of a drama queen. I mean, they weren't even her pants!

"Who's Annabelle Jacobsen?" Dad asked, innocently stirring his vegetables.

"She's a designer," I explained.

"What?" Elise shrieked. "She's *the* designer! The hottest new designer from London! These pants probably cost five hundred dollars! Oh, wait — here's a note." She was about to open it when I plucked it from her fingers.

"I'll handle it, thanks," I said, tearing it open. The card was orange with a white butterfly on the front. Inside was a note in perfectly even, looping script.

"'Thanks for saving me the other night,'" I read aloud. "'Hope this makes your first day at Allington something special! Yours, Jenelle.'"

"How did you save her?" Elise asked.

I quickly filled her in on the stapled hem.

"That *was* good thinking," Elise admitted. "Wow. That one little staple bought you this fabulous outfit! I can't wait to tell Blake!"

"But I already had an outfit planned for the first day of school," I said, sitting down across from Elise.

"What?" Elise gaped at me, her green eyes huge. "Are you nuts? This is the kind of outfit they wear in *It!* magazine! I swear, I think I saw Ashley Violetta in these pants the other day. Wear your other thing on the *second* day!"

I traced a finger across the shirt's soft crinkly cotton. I really did like the fabric, even if the solid color was a little more ho-hum than I usually wear. "Well . . ." I said after a moment. "I guess I don't want to hurt Jenelle's feelings. . . ."

"You'd better not," Elise agreed. "She's your best friend at Allington now."

"Good point." I laughed. Besides, it was really sweet of her to send me such a nice thank-you. I didn't want to seem ungrateful. "Okay, I'll wear the outfit. I'll just find a way to make it a little more . . . me."

Elise folded the pants reverently and nestled them back into their sheets of purple tissue paper. "And just how are you going to do that?"

I grinned at her. "With the magic of accessories!" I explained.

"Oh, jeez." Kirk's spoon clattered into his bright green cereal bowl the minute I walked into the kitchen. "What are you wearing *now*?"

"It's an Annabelle Jacobsen outfit," I told him, looking down at my clothes. "Jenelle gave it to me."

"I think you look darling, sweetie!" Mom said from her place across from Kirk. "That's a great outfit for the first day of school." She took a long pull from her favorite coffee mug, the one that read, COFFEE: IT MAKES EVERYTHING SEEM INTERESTING — EVEN YOU!

"Thanks, Mom." I slid into the seat beside my brother.

"Bacon?" Dad asked from his place at the stove. "Scrambled eggs?"

"I'll have some eggs," I said, and Dad happily poured yellow liquid into the hot pan and started scrambling. Then he popped a slice of bread into the toaster.

"I'm not talking about Amy's *clothes*," Kirk explained, rolling his eyes. He can never just let anything go. "I'm talking about that piece of wack-ness," he said, pointing to the tote I'd dropped beside my chair. It was the size of our microwave and covered in fake flowers. "And that additional insanity," he added, pointing to my shoes — yellow patent-leather Mary Janes that matched my chunky jewelry. I'd taken a risk by wearing the shoes with bright blue socks that went with the flowers on my bag. Personally, I thought it made the whole outfit pop — the pink on pink, the multicolored bag, the bright socks. I'd pulled my hair back into a low ponytail to keep the frizz factor down and, hon-estly, I thought I looked pretty good.

"You look like you just escaped from clown college," Kirk said.

"Like I'm going to take fashion advice from a guy wearing a *Dukes of Hazzard* T-shirt," I said, lift-ing my eyebrows at him. "What are you eating, anyway?" The milk in his bowl was an odd shade of pinkish-brown. And by "odd" I mean "revolting."

"Choco-bites," he said, digging in with his spoon. "Mixed with Fruity Ohs."

I grimaced. "That's disgusting."

He grinned at me. "So are your socks."

"Okay, kids, that's enough," Dad said, placing a plate of toast and eggs in front of me. He'd added some kind of chopped herbs and grated cheese to the eggs. Delicious.

"You've only got ten minutes to get to the bus, and I'm not driving you," Mom warned.

"You hear that?" Kirk said, flicking his shaggy brown hair out of his eyes. "You've still got ten minutes. It's not too late to change your shoes."

"Just eat your fruitochococrisps," I told him.

Kirk and I gobbled the rest of our breakfast. Then he ran upstairs to grab his backpack, and we headed down the block to the edge of the park, where our buses were going to pick us up. There were already a few kids at the stop when we got there, but all of them looked older, like they belonged with my brother.

Kirk goes to Smith, the local high school, and his classes had started the week before. That's why — when his long yellow bus finally rattled up the curb — Kirk's friend Marshall was already leaning out the window shouting, "Kirk! Yo, Kirk!" and waving his arms frantically.

"Tell Marshall that he can get decapitated doing that," I said as Kirk bounded toward the doors.

"Just don't get kidnapped by anyone in a rainbow wig," Kirk called over his shoulder, eyeing my huge bag. "Stay away from guys in big shoes." He cackled and boarded the bus, and the doors clattered closed behind him.

He pounded on the window as the bus lurched away from the curb. He shouted something through the glass, but his voice was muffled.

"What?" I called.

Kirk pulled down the window. "Have fun at Allington!" he shouted. "Beware of the preps!"

I sighed. Sure enough, all of the kids at the bus stop had gotten onto the Smith bus. Now I was standing at the corner by myself, feeling a little conspicuous. I wished that I had a novel in my bag. I had almost everything else — a nail file, hairbrush, mini-stapler, three notebooks, five black pens, three blue pens, two green pens, a purple pen, a tube of Krazy Glue, a pad of paper for homework assignments, my wallet, a packet of tissues, a tube of Mentos, four shades of lip gloss, and a bunch of other stuff I couldn't even remember. I'd sort of transferred everything to the new bag in a hurry. But I'd just finished reading my book and had forgotten to add a new one.

I was debating whether or not to study the ingredients in my Mentos when a humongous bus pulled up in front of me. It wasn't a school bus, though. It was super-tall and had dark-tinted glass — like the buses tourists ride around in. I stepped back just as the doors opened and a perky woman in a hunter-green polo shirt and khaki pants stepped out. She looked down at her clipboard, then up at me. "Amy Flowers?" she asked.

I was so surprised that I just nodded.

The woman flapped her fingers at me in a get-on-the-bus gesture, and that was when I noticed that her polo shirt said ALLINGTON ACADEMY in the upper left corner. It was written on the bus, too, in small, tasteful gold letters near the door. *Whoa — this is my* school *bus? Insanity.*

I climbed the stairs into the shiny, plush interior of the bus. It was clean and cool inside — the air-conditioning felt wonderful. It was still late August in Houston, and although it wasn't even eight in the morning, it was hot.

"Orange or sparkling?" the woman with the ponytail asked as the doors hissed closed and the bus pulled away from the curb.

I thought about that for a moment, but I couldn't make any sense out of the question. "Sorry?"

The woman sighed, as if it was particularly torturous to have to deal with someone as dumb as me this early in the morning. She exaggerated her lip movements and spoke very slowly, "Do you want orange juice or sparkling water?" She pointed to a cooler nearby that was packed with drinks.

"Oh," I said. "Uh, how much does it cost?"

The woman shook her head, like I really was the slowest person on the planet. "They're free," she said, like — duh, of course, doesn't every school bus hand out free beverages on the way to class? "The newspapers are free, too," she added.

"The school gives out newspapers?" I repeated.

"It's a curriculum enrichment program," the woman explained. "The faculty encourages all students to be up on current events. We have *The New York Times* or the *Wall Street Journal*."

"No *Houston Chronicle*?" I asked, surprised.

The woman gave me a you-must-be-joking look.

"I'll take a *Times* and a juice, please," I said quickly. Grabbing my stuff, I slunk to the first empty seat I saw and fiddled with the buttons on the TV screen on the seat back in front of me. This bus was nicer than my *house*! I mean, it had premium cable!

It seemed like only minutes had passed when the bus pulled up to Allington. I'd been there before, of course, for a tour of the campus. But now, with the masses of perfectly groomed students spilling in through the iron front gates and the line of luxury cars waiting to pull up to the entrance, it seemed even bigger and more intimidating than I remembered. The massive mansion-style main building had white columns at the front and acres of manicured green lawns at the back, including playing fields, a track, tennis courts, and a golf course. The front of the building was partially hidden by enormous, leafy oaks, and soft, dappled light fell over the courtyard. A large circular fountain sent out a light spray, which, combined with the shade, made the courtyard pleasantly cool.

Looking up at the large building, my heart gave a little flutter. *This is it,* I thought. *My first day at Allington Academy.* I was scared, but excited, too.

"Watch out!" cried a voice, and all of a sudden I heard a scraping sound, and then a *whoosh* as something brushed against my cheek. Looking down, I saw a girl sprawled at my feet. She had on a fitted olive-green T-shirt with a graphic chicken on it and a pair of new-looking capri jeans. She swung her head, and her chin-length glossy black hair swayed like she was in a shampoo commercial. "Oops," she said as she watched her skateboard roll across the courtyard and come to a stop at the base of a tree. She squinted up at me. "Sorry about that," Glossy-haired Girl said. Half of her mouth twisted up into a smile. "Guess I shouldn't be practicing my grinds in a crowded courtyard."

"No problem," I said, holding out my hand. "Skateboarding is not a crime," I added, repeating the slogan on my brother's favorite bumper sticker — the one he has plastered across his math book.

"Tell that to the administration." The girl took my hand, and I helped haul her to her feet. When she stood up, I saw that she was about my height. "I'm Michiko Ohara," she said. "But everyone calls me Mitchie."

"Amy Flowers," I said.

Mitchie looked up at the fountain. "One day, I'm going to master that thing," she said. "All I want is to get partway around the lip on my skateboard without falling. Or injuring innocent bystanders." Mitchie eyed my tote. "Cool bag." She noticed the *Times* tucked under my arm and smiled faintly. "You took the newspaper."

"What?"

Mitchie shook her head a little. "Did you come on the bus? It's just — people don't usually take the newspaper," she said.

"Oh." I shrugged. "I'll take almost anything any-one gives me," I said. "Especially if it's free."

Mitchie laughed, and I laughed a little, too. "Well, I guess I'll see you around." With a little wave, Mitchie hustled after her skateboard.

"See you," I called. Then, with a deep breath, I headed up the white marble steps and into the main building of Allington Academy.

The white marble hall gleamed as students streamed past, checking the schedules in their hands against the classroom listings posted on the enormous flat-screen monitors that lined the walls. At the center of the hall was a marble stair-case the width of a city bus. I felt like I'd just walked into a fairy-tale castle — only it was a parallel universe in which *everyone* looked like Cinderella and Prince Charming. A teacher walked by, her hair in a perfect golden bun at the back of her neck. She had on black heels, a red flared skirt, and a white silk shirt. She was holding a biology textbook. At my old school, my science teacher came to class in flip-flops.

I dug around in my bag and finally came up with my student ID and schedule. The ID was pale blue plastic and had Allington's crest, a screaming gold eagle, in the upper right corner. A lot of stores here in Houston give Allington students a discount. Which is kind of ironic, since they're probably the richest kids in town.

I scanned my schedule. HOMEROOM, it read, MS. MANNING. I looked up at the monitors, searching the Ms. ROOM M104. I had no idea where that was, but I took a guess and headed to the right.

I was just passing by a bank of pale blue lockers when I spotted a familiar blond head. "Jenelle!" I called. "Hey, Jenelle!"

Jenelle was standing with two other girls. One was — ugh — Fiona, of course. The other was someone I'd never seen before. She had long, wavy brown hair and wore a lavender empire-waisted shirt and black skirt that really flattered her curvy figure. Jenelle and Fiona had on almost exactly the same thing as the other girl — in different colors. Fiona's shirt was blue, and Jenelle's was peach. Each of them also wore a wristful of gold bangles. *Did they plan that?* I wondered. *Or are they so on the same fashion wavelength that they ended up dressing like triplets?*

"Hi, Amy," Jenelle said, smiling. "Great! You wore the outfit!" Then her eyes landed on my tote bag, and her smile sort of froze in place. It looked like someone had stuck it on her, like a plastic Mrs. Potato Head mouth.

"Yeah, thanks so much for sending it over," I

told her. "I love it." I resisted the urge to apologize for my bag and decided to change the subject instead. "I just love y'all's bangles."

"Lucia's mother got them for us," Jenelle explained. "First-day-of-school present."

"I'm surprised you like them." Fiona cocked her head. "It seems like you go for more . . . *unusual* accessories."

"Yeah," the girl with the long brown hair — Lucia, I guessed — put in. "Like, very unusual?" She raised her voice at the end of the sentence, which made it sound like a question. But it wasn't a question — it was a definite statement. She was looking at my socks, her lip curled.

Fiona and the girl tickled each other's fingertips in some kind of secret handshake.

Jenelle's cheeks had turned slightly pink. "Amy, this is Lucia de Leon," she said. "And you've already met Fiona."

Yeah, unfortunately, I thought, but what I said was, "Nice to meet you, Lucia."

"Oh, how *cute*," Fiona said. "Look, Lucia, Amy took the newspaper." She smiled a tight little smile and twirled a lock of hair around her finger. "Nobody ever takes the newspaper."

"Yeah, I've never heard of anyone, like, *ever*

taking the newspaper?" Lucia agreed, flipping her long brown waves over her shoulder.

"Why not?" I asked, but Fiona just gave me this look — like she felt sorry for me for even asking.

"Well, I guess we'll see you later, Amy." Fiona flickered a tiny wave in my direction. "Let us know if you read about any fascinating current events."

"Yeah, like, keep us informed?" Lucia agreed, and she and Fiona started off, giggling. Jenelle paused a minute. I couldn't really read the expression on her face — it was like she wanted to apologize to me and yell at me all at the same time.

Finally, she turned and followed her friends, leaving me alone in the hall at Allington Academy with no idea how to get to room M104.

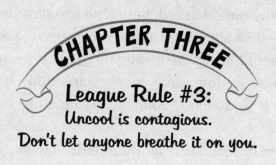

CHAPTER THREE

League Rule #3:
Uncool is contagious.
Don't let anyone breathe it on you.

Oh, ugh, I thought as the bell chimed for third period. I flipped my English book closed and tucked my notebook beneath it. I looked behind me, to the fifth row, where Jenelle and her friends had nabbed seats next to one another. But they had already disappeared. I guess I shouldn't have been so surprised. They'd managed to do that after first period, too. At the beginning of each period, they breezed into the room one nano-second before the chime sounded to start class, and left the instant it gonged to end it. I wasn't really sure what they did between classes, because I looked for them in the halls but never saw them.

And when I did see them, it was like I'd suddenly become invisible to them — and to everyone else. I'd tried giving some of the other kids in the class a smile, but they either ignored me or gave me weird looks. Allington, I was learning, was not exactly Friendlytown.

This isn't how I pictured my first day, I thought. Tucking my books under my arm, I hauled myself to my feet. Time for my next class — Texas history. I wasn't looking forward to it. Not that I have anything against learning about the history of Texas. In fact, Texas has a pretty interesting history. It's the only state that used to be its own country, for example. No — it wasn't the *class* I was dreading. It was the Walk of Shame.

It turns out that just walking down the hall at Allington is practically a social event. Everyone heads from class to class in pairs or clumps, chatting and joking. Even the nerds walk each other to class. I'd never been the new kid at a school before, and I was learning something important — it isn't easy. I felt like a tiny island in a swirling ocean of students.

Okay, where am I going? I thought, burying my nose in my schedule. *Texas history, room A207,* I'd scribbled on my schedule. I hurried up the stairs and started toward room 207, but the minute I stepped up to the door, I could tell it wasn't the right place. The sign on the door read WELCOME TO EIGHTH GRADE ENGLISH! and the kids at the desks looked older than me. Still, the number on the door said 207. . . .

I hesitated a moment, unsure what to do. I decided to check the monitors downstairs. *Maybe there's been a room change*, I thought. I turned quickly — and immediately smashed into someone. Books and papers flew everywhere.

"Oh, I'm so sorry!" I said, reaching for the nearest book.

Unfortunately, the boy I'd smashed into reached for it at the same time.

"Ouch!" he said as our heads cracked together.

"Oh — jeez!" I rubbed my forehead. "Are you okay?"

"Well, I'm in pain, and I'm about to be late for my class. But other than that, I'm great." And that was when the boy looked up at me — and I realized that I knew him. Those warm brown eyes, that soft-looking hair. "Hey . . ." he said slowly. "Aren't you that girl from the CD store?"

My cheeks felt hot, and I instantly knew that I was blushing, which only made me blush harder. See, I don't blush like a normal person — I get a bright red blotch on each of my cheeks, and in the center of each blotch is a white patch. It looks ridiculous. Kirk always calls it "Amy's Gotcha Bull's-eye."

But if the cute boy noticed, he didn't say anything. "It's you, right? You picked out that CD for my mom."

I nodded. *Say something*, I commanded myself. *Okay,* I thought, *but what?*

"I'm Scott Lawton." The boy picked up a book and frowned at it. "This is yours, I think. Anyway, my mom loved the CD. Angelina Fry is her new favorite singer — she's already downloaded all of her other albums."

"Really?" I squeaked. I cleared my throat. I hadn't meant to sound that excited. "That's — that's great. I'm Amy, by the way. Amy Flowers."

"Great to meet you, Amy." Scott grinned, and I couldn't help admiring his teeth. They were white and perfectly even. *I'll bet he never even needed braces*, I thought, running my tongue over the backs of the silver bonds on my bottom teeth.

We finished gathering our books and stood up. My head felt light, but I took this as a good sign. As long as it didn't feel as if a five-alarm fire was going off on my face, it meant I probably wasn't blushing anymore.

"So . . ." Scott jerked his head in the direction of the class behind him. "Is this where you're headed?"

"No — actually, I'm not sure where I'm going," I admitted. I held out my schedule. "This says 207, but this doesn't seem to be the right room."

Scott took the paper from my hand, and — for a split second — his finger brushed against mine. It sent a chill up my spine and all the way across my scalp. Whoa. I'd never felt *that* before.

But if an electric current had just jolted through Scott, he didn't show it. He just glanced quickly at the schedule, then looked up at me. "You're supposed to be in room *A*207," he said. He put extra emphasis on the A, as if that explained everything.

"Oh, right," I said, feeling like an idiot. "And — um — where's A?"

"It's the Austin Building — directly behind this one," Scott explained. "Just go out the rear doors, and there's a covered walkway that leads right to it. You're lucky to have a class there — that's the nice building. Everything's new."

"*That's* the nice building?" I repeated, looking around at the pristine marble floors, the carved wooden moldings, the fresh paint. "At my old school, the hallways smelled like feet." Instantly, I bit my lip. Sometimes, I say things out loud before I have a chance to say them in my head and think about how gross they might sound.

Scott laughed. "Well, the Austin Building has a brand-new climate system with odor control. The whole place smells like baby powder."

"Seriously? This place is too much."

Scott shrugged. "Welcome to Allington," he said simply. "Listen, you'd better hurry. You've only got two minutes until the bell."

I looked at my watch and let out a little gasp. He was right! "Thanks for the help." Turning, I hustled toward the stairs. The halls were already nearly deserted.

"Same to you," Scott called.

I waved and bolted down the stairs. But it wasn't just the thought of being late that had my heart pounding. *Scott Lawton*, I thought as I flung open the rear doors and darted down the covered walkway. *CD Store Boy is right here — at Allington! And he was nice to me!*

Suddenly, I felt like this whole day might just turn around.

I slipped into my desk with thirty seconds to spare and looked around the room. As usual, I was sitting in a little puddle of aloneness: The desks around me were empty. With a sigh, I pulled out a new notebook. The pages crackled slightly as I opened it for the first time. I always love that sound.

I felt someone move into the chair beside me, and when I looked up, I saw Jenelle digging around in her handbag. Finally, she came up with a pen. She looked at me and smiled. "Hi," she said just as the bell chimed.

"Awright class." An older man with glasses and a military haircut stood up at the front of the room. "Let's get started. My name is Mr. Burgess. Anyone who does not belong in seventh-grade Texas history should leave right now." He folded his arms across his chest and waited, leaning against his desk. Nobody moved. "Well, looks like we've got a right smart group this year," he said. "I guess I can start handing out y'all's books." I couldn't help noticing that the muscles in his arms rippled when he gestured. For an old guy, Mr. Burgess was in incredible shape.

He sat down behind his desk and called roll. I noticed Jenelle scribbling madly, and a moment later, her foot was tracing a delicate arc toward my desk. Beneath the pointed toe of her mule was the edge of a folded piece of paper. I dropped my pen and bent to get the note, unfolding it carefully behind my notebook as Mr. Burgess called the first student, Anthony Adams, to come and get his book and packet of supplies.

The books, by the way, were brand-new and *given* to students — not on loan, the way they always had been in public school. That meant I could write in mine, take notes, highlight, whatever. Some of the kids in my earlier classes had already started scribbling on the covers of theirs, but I knew I'd never do that. I couldn't. It just seemed wrong. It would be hard enough to get myself to underline something after six years of being told not to.

I smoothed the note with my palm, feeling a strange mixture of annoyance and relief that Jenelle was writing me now. After all, she'd ignored me the rest of the morning, when she was with her friends. But now that Fiona and Lucia were nowhere to be found, she wanted to chat? I looked down at the note.

What's your cell number? it read. *I'll text you.*

No cell, I wrote, dropping the note on the floor. When Jenelle read it, she made a little squeaking noise.

"Is everything all right, Ms. Renwick?" Mr. Burgess asked, peering at her over the tops of his glasses.

43

Jenelle cleared her throat. "Sorry, Mr. Burgess," she said quickly. "I have a cough."

The teacher just nodded and called out, "Monique Duvall."

After a moment, Jenelle delivered a new note:

I've barely seen you in our other classes! Fiona always spends the whole passing period in the bathroom. You should come with us next time.

I clicked my pen open and closed, feeling a warm rush of relief wash through me. So Jenelle wasn't avoiding me.

No wonder her lip gloss always looks perfect, I wrote back.

Mr. Burgess called my name, and I dropped the note on the floor as I made my way to the front of the class. When I got back to my seat, a new note was waiting on my desk for me:

Fiona says you can sit with us at lunch. If you leave your bag in your locker.

There was a face with a squiggly line for a mouth at the end of the note. I looked down at my bag. *Is it really that bad?* I thought. I mean, I still thought it was cool. I glanced over at Jenelle, and she winced. "Sorry," she mouthed. She started scribbling a new note. She waited for Mr. Burgess to look down at his list, then tossed it over to my desk.

I know Fiona can be a pain, it read. *She likes to have things her way, especially around people she doesn't know well. But she's really sweet once you get to know her. Promise.*

Hmm, I thought. *Maybe Jenelle has a point. I haven't really given Fiona a chance — maybe she's just got a weird sense of humor. And Jenelle is really nice.* Besides, who else was I going to sit with? I mean, I'd had a conversation with Scott Lawton, but I wasn't exactly about to go plop my lunch bag down next to him in the cafeteria. *Okay,* I wrote at last. *Cool.*

Jenelle wrote something else, dropping it onto my desk as she stood up to retrieve her book and supply bag from the front of the room:

And you might want to take off your socks. They don't exactly go with the rest of the outfit.

I narrowed my eyes. She wanted me to get rid of my *socks*? That seemed ridiculous. I was just about to write *no way* when I stopped. *Actually,* I thought, *if I put my bag in my locker, the socks really won't go with the rest of my outfit. I'll have on a rose shirt, pink pants, yellow shoes, and blue socks.*

Jenelle slipped back into her seat. She flipped open her book, then cast a sideways glance at me. She smiled a little, like she was hoping that I'd say yes.

I sighed as thoughts poured down on me like rain. *Do I really want to cause drama between Jenelle and Fiona? She's known Fiona for a long time, and she only met me a week ago. At least she's trying to be my friend. And maybe Fiona really isn't as bad as she seems. . . .*

Okay, I wrote finally, and passed the note back to Jenelle.

I didn't like it, but I didn't know what else to do.

It's just one lunch, I told myself. *One sockless, bagless lunch. I can live with that.*

Right?

"Okay, well think about it!" A group of really pretty girls was clustered around Jenelle's table when I arrived. The tallest one — she was gorgeous, with smooth skin the color of coffee with cream — was talking to Fiona. "We'd love it if you guys would try out for the cheer squad."

A smile hovered at the corners of Fiona's glossy lips. "I'm not really much of a joiner. But maybe Jenelle and Lucia would think about it." The way she said it made it sound incredibly unlikely.

"Well, let us know if you change your mind." The cheerleaders walked off, looking slightly deflated.

46

"Hey, Amy," Jenelle said, catching sight of me. It had taken me a little while to find them. The Allington cafeteria wasn't just one big warehouse-style space, like at my old school. Here, the cafeteria — the dining hall — was made up of a bunch of smaller rooms, branching out from the food service area. Each room was painted in a unique style and named after a flower. This was the Dahlia Room. The walls were a warm, dark maroon lined with windows that looked out onto the lush green school grounds. A crystal chandelier hung from the center of the ceiling over tables of dark wood and chairs with plush maroon cushions. All in all, it was a nice place to have lunch. Like, the nicest place I'd ever been.

Jenelle, Fiona, and Lucia had a prime table by the windows farthest from the entrance. The table was long enough to seat eight. I set my brown bag down on the table and took the seat beside Jenelle and across from Lucia. "How's everyone's first day going?" I asked as I pulled my lunch out of the bag.

Fiona rolled her eyes. "The first day is always such a waste," she griped. "You spend all of your time getting your books and looking over the syllabus. I mean, couldn't they just deliver all of that to our houses and give us the day off?"

"Yeah, right?" Lucia agreed. She poked her fork delicately at the salad on the plate in front of her. "Like, I'd rather have the day off?"

Just then, a couple of girls appeared at the end of the table. They looked younger than us — maybe sixth graders — and one of them, a girl with a cloud of short curly blond hair, set her tray at the place at the corner. Fiona snapped her fingers at her. "Excuse me," she said. "What do you think you're doing?"

The girl with the curly hair touched her chest lightly, and her eyebrows flew up. She shot a nervous glance at her friend, who was gaping at Fiona with huge black eyes.

"Yes, *you*," Fiona snapped. "This is our table. No sixthies. Find your own spot."

The sixth graders didn't even whimper. They just grabbed their trays and scampered out of the room, as if someone had set their feet on fire.

"I swear, who do these sixthies think they *are*?" Lucia asked, glaring after them.

"It's just sad," Fiona agreed, shaking her head.

"They have no clue," Jenelle put in.

I was about to say that there was plenty of room at the end of the table, but decided against it. After all, everyone else seemed to think it was some kind

48

of criminal offense for them to want to sit beside us. *I guess that's the way things are done here*, I told myself as I unwrapped my sandwich.

"Omigosh, what is *that*?" Fiona demanded just as I was about to take a bite.

I blinked at her in surprise. "A sandwich?"

"I can *see* it's a sandwich," Fiona snapped. She waved her hand delicately in front of her nose. "But what's that *smell*?"

"Yeah — what *is* it?" Lucia demanded, wrinkling her nose.

"Liverwurst," I said.

"And what are *those*?" Fiona asked, pointing to my bag of chips with a long manicured nail. But she answered her own question before I could. "Potato chips. And a Coke."

"Is she *serious*?" Lucia asked Jenelle. Like I wasn't even there.

"What's wrong with my lunch?" I asked.

"What's wrong with eating one giant brick of fat?" Fiona demanded. Sarcasm oozed out of her voice like the filling in a jelly doughnut. "Um, nothing — if you want to join the Grease Patrol." She grimaced at my lunch, as if the sight of it offended her.

"You've got to get rid of it," Jenelle said simply. Reaching out, she grabbed my sandwich and stuffed it back into my lunch bag. Then she took the chips, and before I could even stop her, she was across the room, tossing my food into the elegant garbage can in the corner.

"*Thank* you," Fiona said when Jenelle returned to the table. She made it sound as if Jenelle had just participated in a toxic-waste cleanup.

"What am I supposed to eat now?" I demanded. Anger simmered through my body — I felt myself starting to get hot.

Fiona snorted. "A pile of napkins would be healthier than that disaster you brought."

"Yeah, like, it would have more fiber?" Lucia added.

"Just go get something from the buffet," Jenelle suggested.

"I don't have any money," I pointed out. I was too polite to mention that I'd been forced to leave my purse back in my locker so as not to offend Fiona's delicate sensibilities.

Jenelle just looked at me for a moment. Then she started to crack up. The other girls did, too.

"What's so funny?" I demanded. *My potential death by starvation?*

"You don't need money," Jenelle explained. "Just go up and take what you want."

"Really?"

Fiona shrugged. "It's all covered in your tuition. Go see for yourself."

I'm starting to see why Allington is the most expensive school in the state, I thought as I shoved back my chair. But when I stepped into the food service area, I realized that Fiona and Jenelle might just be telling the truth — there were no cash registers anywhere.

Grabbing one of the hexagonal black trays, I took a quick gourmet tour. Everything was in its own little section — there was a pasta bar, a baked potato bar, a breakfast cereal bar, a drink bar, a salad bar, an entrée bar, even a dessert bar. That's where I paused.

"The cookies are way better," said a voice beside my ear as I reached for a bowl of rice pudding.

Mitchie was standing right behind me.

"Really?" I asked. "What's so special about the cookies?"

"They're the best in town!" Mitchie looked surprised — as if Allington cookies were world-famous. "The oatmeal raisins were just written up in *Texas Magazine*."

"Sounds like my kind of dessert," I said, exchanging my pudding for an oatmeal-raisin cookie.

"Where are you sitting?" Mitchie asked. "Want to join me and my friends? We're in the Sunflower Room." She gestured behind her.

"Actually, I'm in the Dahlia," I told her. "At the table by the windows."

Mitchie's eyebrows drew together. "That's the League's table."

"The what?"

"The League — Fiona Von Steig and her crew. Is that who you're sitting with?" She blinked at me, her face doubtful.

"Jenelle is . . ." But I wasn't sure what to say. My friend? My almost-cousin? My dad's best friend's future stepdaughter? I gave up. "They call themselves the League?" I asked. "Why?"

"They don't call *themselves* that," Mitchie corrected. "Everyone *else* calls them that. As in, 'They're out of your league.'" Her eyes narrowed slightly. "If you're sitting with them, you don't want to eat this," she said, taking the tiny plate that held my cookie and putting it back on the dessert bar.

"Yeah — they kind of just chucked out my liverwurst sandwich, too," I said.

"Liverwurst? Oh wow." Mitchie shook her head.

I sighed. "Well, what *can* I eat?"

Mitchie pursed her lips and nodded in the direction of the salad bar. "Go for a chicken Caesar, no croutons, a bag of Air Crisps, and — here." Turning, she yanked open a cooler and pulled out a green glass bottle of sparkling water.

"Thanks," I said uncertainly.

But Mitchie had already started walking away.

I served myself a salad and took a bag of Air Crisps off the rack, then made my way back to the Dahlia Room.

"So, do you think you can come to my pool party?" A really handsome older guy was standing beside Fiona, who was scanning something that looked like an invitation. "You're all invited," he added, turning to include Jenelle and Lucia.

"Sounds interesting," Fiona told him. "We'll try to make it."

The guy grinned and hurried off, looking as if he couldn't wait to go tell someone that he'd just won the megabucks lottery jackpot.

"That's better," Fiona said when I sat down with my tray.

Better — for who? I thought as I picked up my heavy, silver fork. Still, I had to admit that the salad was delicious. The chicken was tender, and the dressing was garlicky and creamy, not too gloppy.

"So, Amy . . ." Fiona tucked the pool party invitation into her bag and looked at me from beneath glossy black lashes. "Got any crushes yet?"

"Fiona, she's only been here half a day," Jenelle said.

"That's plenty of time to spot someone crush-worthy," Fiona replied. "Besides, look at her — she's blushing like a giant Target sign."

It was true; I could feel it.

"So, who is it?" Fiona asked. "Spill."

I hesitated. "Scott Lawton," I said finally.

Fiona looked blank. "Who?"

"He's this guy I met in a CD store," I said. "I just ran into him — I think he's in eighth."

"I've never heard of him," Fiona said.

"Me neither?" Lucia agreed.

"You should go for someone popular," Fiona suggested. "Someone in our grade. It's easier; you have more to talk about. And with your coloring . . . I think you'd look good with a blond-haired guy." She took a delicate sip of her sparkling water and placed the glass back on the tray with a slight click. "Someone like Anderson Sempe."

"Fiona!" Jenelle looked shocked. Her hazel eyes were huge. It was obvious that this Anderson — whoever he was — was *Jenelle's* crush.

"Don't get bent out of shape," Fiona said calmly. She made a kissy face at Jenelle. "You know it doesn't make sense for you to go for Anderson. You and he are the same height. If you wear heels, you'll look ridiculous. Let Amy go for him."

Jenelle stabbed at the piece of grilled salmon on her plate, but she didn't say anything. I wanted to tell her that it was okay — that I didn't even know who Anderson was. But I didn't want to get in the middle of a fight between Jenelle and Fiona. I decided I'd pull Jenelle aside later.

"Don't be mad," Fiona said smoothly. "Look, I have something that will cheer you up." She pulled a DVD case out of her bag. On the cover was a gorgeous photo of the League. YOU'RE IN, read the title.

"Omigosh, I look, like, hideous in that picture?" Lucia said.

"What are you talking about?" Jenelle demanded. "You look amazing. I'm the one who looks like I'm about to sneeze. I can't believe you're going to hand that out to everybody."

I squinted at the photo. As far as I could tell, the three of them looked like professional models.

"I'm not handing it out to *everybody*," Fiona corrected. "Not by a long shot."

"What's it for?" I asked.

Fiona opened the case and pulled out a silver DVD. "It's an invitation to my thirteenth birthday party," she explained. "It's going to be the biggest bash of the year."

"Of, like, the decade?" Lucia agreed, gathering her long hair over one shoulder and raking her fingers through the silky waves. "Of, like, the millennium?"

Jenelle nodded. "Fiona's been planning it for months. It's going to be really amazing. She's rented out a whole club. The theme is 'Winter Wonderland,' and there's going to be a DJ and even a private performance by Eloquence."

"The band?" I asked. I'd heard a few of their songs on the radio — they were really good.

"My dad is their lawyer," Fiona explained.

"She even had, like, a professional director make the video invitation?" Lucia informed me. "He's Steven Spielberg's cousin?"

"Wow," I said. "What should I wear?"

Fiona looked at me, her blue eyes glittering like sapphires. "I don't even know you," she pointed out. "Jenelle is the one who has to be nice to you, not me. If you want to come to my party, you'll have to *earn* your way in." She placed the DVD back in its case and snapped it closed.

I stared at her. *Earn* my way in? How obnoxious. Part of me wanted to tell her to go take a leap.

But another part of me wanted to go to that party. . . .

At that moment, the bell chimed. The League gathered their purses and left their trays on the table. I left mine, too, even though it felt strange not to clean up after myself.

Jenelle didn't meet my eyes as we filed out of the Dahlia Room. That was okay with me. I was starting to wonder if she'd told me the truth when she said that Fiona could be really sweet once you got to know her. So far, it just didn't seem possible.

I had to dash to my locker to grab my bag and my books before my next class, science. When I got there, Jenelle and Fiona were already seated at a lab table near the back. I hesitated for a moment, and then walked over to join them. After all, Jenelle had said I should.

"It's two to a lab table," Fiona said the minute I walked up to them. She was writing in a notebook and didn't bother looking up to talk to me.

Jenelle shrugged. "Sorry."

"Why don't you sit at *that* table?" Fiona suggested, pointing toward the front of the room where a cute boy with curly blond hair had just plopped his books down.

Jenelle shifted in her seat uncomfortably and looked like she was about to say something. But then she cast a glance at Fiona and seemed to change her mind.

Just then, the teacher walked in and I had to find a spot. Fiona's suggestion was as good as any, so I walked up to the cute boy and said, "Is it okay if I sit here?"

He looked up at me and smiled. He had wide blue eyes and a grin that was pure Hollywood. "Sure," he said. "Are you new? I'm Anderson Sempe."

"Anderson?" I repeated, glancing at Fiona. She was smiling at me.

"I know, I know, what kind of name is that, right?" Anderson looked sheepish. "It was my grandmother's maiden name. They do that in my family."

"Oh, I didn't mean —" I shook my head, unsure how to explain myself without sounding like a total nerd. "I'm Amy Flowers," I said, placing my bag on the floor and taking the seat next to his.

"Are you any good at science?" Anderson asked. He sounded really hopeful.

I don't usually brag, but this was such a direct question that I didn't know how to answer it without either a) lying, or b) sounding conceited. "I'm pretty good," I told him, going for the compromise.

Anderson looked relieved. "Great," he said. "I've got a ton of friends in this class, but nobody wants to sit with me because they know I'm *lousy* at science." He laughed a little, as if "lousy" didn't begin to cover it.

I looked over my shoulder at Fiona, who was still grinning Cheshire cat–style. Terrific. She'd just stuck me with a lousy lab partner.

Anderson followed my gaze. "Oh, hey — do you know Jenelle and Fiona?" he asked. His voice got a little softer, and he added, "They're nice."

Nice? I thought, but then I noticed that he was looking at Jenelle when he said it, not Fiona. Jenelle blushed a little and instantly peered down into her handbag as if there was some kind of important nuclear secret buried in there that she had to discover right away.

Hmm. . . . *Interesting*.

The bell rang and the teacher — Mr. Pearl — stood up from behind his desk. "All right people, all right, all right, all right!" He had a potbelly and wore his tie a little too short, which made him look like the picture of Papa Bear from my old copy of *Goldilocks*. He had dark skin and huge eyes, and when he talked, he opened them wide and gestured enthusiastically, like he'd had about twelve cups of coffee. He clapped his hands together. "Welcome to science! We're going to get started right away working with magnets. Who knows anything about magnets? Anyone? Anyone? Anyone?"

A girl with a stylish haircut raised her hand and said something about positive and negative charges, and soon Mr. Pearl was flashing a PowerPoint presentation on a screen at the front of the class. I wrote down what he said. Even though I was just writing down what was on the screen, Anderson kept leaning over to look at my notes.

"Okay, everyone, homework assignment!" Mr. Pearl shouted five minutes before the bell rang.

The class let out a groan.

"I know, I know, I know — what am I doing giving a homework assignment on the first day of class?" Mr. Pearl's eyes nearly bugged out of his head. "I'm crazy, people, I know it! Get used to it! Okay, here it is — come up with an experiment using magnets, and try it out! That's it! Grab a few of these magnets on the way out and see what you can come up with, okay? Okay? Okay? Okay? Thinking caps, people!"

"I hate homework assignments like this," Anderson muttered as he copied the assignment from my notebook. "Why can't he just tell us what to do?"

"Hmm," I said, but I was actually thinking about how much I like it when teachers give out creative assignments. Last year, my science teacher just had us copy vocabulary out of the book and define it. Thrilling.

Anderson ran his hands through his hair, pulling his bangs back and exposing his long eyelashes. Without his hair, his eyes looked even larger — and bluer. *He really is cute,* I thought. I could see why Jenelle liked him. I mean, he wasn't exactly the sharpest blade of grass on the lawn, but he was nice. And gorgeous.

Still, he wasn't my type. *But maybe I could find out if he likes Jenelle,* I thought. After all, there was that look he gave her at the beginning of class. . . . And if he does like her back, then Fiona's secret plan won't matter.

Anderson rested his elbows on our lab table. "What am I going to do?" he muttered.

"About what?" I asked, wondering if he'd some-how read my mind about Fiona's evil plan.

"About the magnets! I have no clue." He shook his head.

"Well . . ." I thought for a moment. "Maybe you could try to figure out whether heat and cold have any effect on the magnet. Like, is it stronger if it's warm? I think that's what I'll do. You could do the same thing."

Anderson sat up straight. "Amy, that's great! I'll stick the magnet in the microwave and see what happens." He started writing that down in his notebook.

"Wait, wait, hold on." I put my hand over his, to stop the scribbling. "Um . . . I think that might blow up your microwave."

"Really?" For a moment, Anderson looked shocked. Then, slowly, he crossed out *Put magnet in microwave.* He had really even handwriting. I was surprised — most guys I know have handwrit-ing that looks like high-priced abstract art.

"Why don't you just leave the magnet in the sun?" I suggested. "And then you could put it in the fridge."

Worry crossed his face like a cloud. "You don't think I'll blow up the fridge, do you?"

I started to laugh, but then I saw that he was serious, and I had to clear my throat to wipe the smile off my face. "No," I said finally. "I think the fridge will be fine."

Anderson nodded and wrote down both of my suggestions. "It's so lucky that I found you," he said, smiling up at me. "I've got a good feeling about this class."

I snuck a glance over my shoulder, and caught Jenelle watching Anderson. When she saw me, she started scribbling in her assignment book. I smiled. "I have a really good feeling, too," I told him.

"Jenelle!" I called, hurrying over to where she was standing beside her yellow locker. I just had time to catch a glimpse of the inside — books and spiral-bound notebooks lined up neatly with their spines facing outward, a rose-colored book bag on the top shelf, and photos of her friends inside the door — before she slammed it shut. When she turned to face me, her expression was entirely neutral, like the outside of her locker. I wondered what she was thinking.

"Hey, Jenelle," I said, feeling a little breathless. "Listen, I just wanted to tell you that I think

Anderson was kind of looking at you all through science." I grinned at her. I just love sharing good news.

For a moment, her expression didn't change. And then, all of a sudden it did, and it was like the sun appearing at the edge of the horizon. Her face flushed pink and her eyes widened. "Really?" she said. "No, you're lying."

"I'm not," I told her. "I thought he was going to give himself whiplash, I swear!"

"Really?" she said again, her voice dreamy.

"Yeah." I nodded. "Really."

Jenelle leaned against her locker, pressing the side of her forehead onto its cool surface. After a few moments, she seemed to remember that I was there, and she straightened up. "Listen, I wanted to tell you something. About what Fiona said at lunch."

"About my liverwurst sandwich?" I asked.

A little smile, almost as invisible as a thin curl of smoke, threatened to take shape at the corner of her mouth. "Um, no," she said. "She said that I have to be nice to you — you know, because your dad is friends with Steve. I just wanted you to know . . ." Jenelle pressed her lips together. "I just wanted you to know that I don't have to. Be nice to you, I mean. That is, that's not why I'm talking to you. In case you wondered." She hitched her slouchy leather bag higher onto her shoulder and left her thumb there, between her shoulder and the strap, as if she'd forgotten what to do with it.

"I didn't think so," I said, although I have to admit that I was glad to hear her say that. "And that's not why I'm being nice to you either," I told her. "In case you were wondering."

She really did smile, then. "Good," she said. For a moment, we just looked at each other. "Hey!" she said suddenly. "What are you doing right now?"

I checked my watch, and my eyeballs nearly fell onto the floor. "Yikes! I'm running for the bus."

I started to turn away, but Jenelle grabbed my elbow. "Do you want to come with me? Lucia and I are helping Fiona pass out invitations to her party." She looked over her shoulder, as if she was afraid that someone might overhear what she was about to say next. "Listen, if you help, I'll bet Fiona will give you an invite." When I hesitated, she added, "Seriously, it would be so much fun if you could come to the party."

I could still feel the pressure of her fingers wrapped around my arm. Jenelle really looked like she meant it. "Okay," I said at last. "I just have to call my mom and tell her I'll be home late."

"Great!" Releasing me from her grip, Jenelle

clapped her hands in excitement. She stood there for a moment, waiting for me to do something.

"Um . . . could I borrow your cell phone?" I asked.

"Oh — right!" Jenelle dug it out of her bag and handed it over. It was the latest iPhone model, and I had no clue how to use it. Jenelle had to dial it for me.

One of these days, I thought as the phone rang in my ear, *I'm going to figure out how everything works at this school.*

I hope.

Fiona did not look happy when Jenelle and I walked up to her car. *Then again, Fiona hardly ever looks happy*, I reasoned. She and Lucia were already sitting in the backseat, and Fiona had a little dog on her lap. It was a long-haired Chihuahua, and its fur was almost as silky as Anderson Sempe's hair. The dog's forelock was held back in a pink bow and it had on a diamond collar.

"Oooh, who's the cute little baby?" I asked, reaching through the window to pet the dog on the head. "Who's this sweet girl?"

The tiny dog let out a growl and snapped at me. I pulled back just in time to keep all ten fingers.

"This is Fernando," Fiona said. "He doesn't like . . ." She hunted for the right word. ". . . *strange* people."

Lucia leaned forward with "Like, duh?" written all over her face. "Yeah," she chimed in, "and Fernando isn't, like, a girl?"

And he isn't sweet either, I added silently.

"Fiona, Amy's going to help hand out invites," Jenelle said as she scrambled into the backseat.

"Oh, how *cute*." Fiona fiddled with the ends of her hair. "That'll be fun for you, Amy."

I hung back for a moment. There really wasn't room for me in the backseat. I'd sort of expected Fiona to get picked up from school in a limo, but this car was only a little bigger than normal. Still, it was a really beautiful car — very classic-looking. Rolls Royce, the silver medallion on the front said.

"You can sit in the front," Fiona informed me.

I yanked open the door and slid into the seat beside a college-age kid with freckles half hidden beneath a tan. His hair was a really dark shade of red, bordering on brown. He smiled at me.

"I'm Amy," I said. "Are you Fiona's brother?" I asked, and everyone in the backseat cracked up. Fiona positively cackled, evil genius–style.

The redhead laughed, too, but not in a mean

way. "I'm Jake. Fiona's mother's personal assistant," he explained.

"Oh," I said, nodding as if all of my relatives had personal assistants.

"Are you ready for the big event today?" Jake asked. "I hear this invitation is nearly impossible to get."

"That's what they tell me," I said.

Jake and I chatted for a while. He told me about college — he was a student at Rice University — and I told him that my father was a professor there. "What program?" Jake asked.

"Architecture," I told him. "But he's on sabbatical for a year."

"Cool." Jake nodded. "I'm an English major, but I'll keep an eye out for him. Professor Flowers, right?"

"Right," I said.

"Excuse me," Fiona said from the backseat, "but would you mind cutting the chat session and turning on the iPod?"

Jake gave me a sideways glance, but he reached out to turn on the music.

"Turn it *up*, please," Fiona demanded, and after that, we didn't get a chance to talk much.

After about ten minutes, we pulled onto a street that was absolutely crowded with cars and people. Kids were massed outside of an enormous iron gate, desperate to get onto the manicured lawn of the mansion behind. "Whoa," I said, "who lives *there*?"

Fiona snorted. "*I* do," she said, leaning forward in her seat. She didn't add "you moron," but I could tell she wanted to. "Jake, pull around to the side entrance."

With a nod, Jake turned the corner. He pressed a button and the side gate swung open. Wow. Fiona's house was *massive*. As we pulled toward a garage that was bigger than my house, I got a peek at the crystal blue pool, which was surrounded by tall flowers and elegant, sweeping grasses. At one end was a covered patio and another small house that I guessed was for guests.

"It was nice meeting you, Amy," Jake said as I stepped out of the car. I gave him a wave, then followed the League to the front of the house. A long, stone walkway led from the steps to the house to the front gate, where hundreds of kids were pressed against the iron bars. On either side of the walkway was a beautiful green carpet of thin, soft grass bordered by small red flowers. Someone had set up a table at the top of the marble steps. It was covered with a royal blue tablecloth, and a large vase of blue flowers was set in the center.

"Oh, I love that color," I said as we walked up to the table. I touched the hem of the cloth and was surprised at how soft the material was.

"Fiona's birthstone is sapphire?" Lucia explained as Fiona pulled a cardboard box from beneath the table. "That's why she always wears something blue?"

"Okay, Jenelle," Fiona said, pulling a clipboard from the top of the box. "Here's your list of names. You've got A to Q. Lucia is doing R to Z. If the person's name is on the list, just check it off and hand them a DVD." I have to admit, I was pretty impressed by Fiona's organization. And the crowd at her gates didn't seem to make her nervous in the slightest. If those were my friends, I'd be stressed about making them wait outside. It was hot, after all. But that was one thing about Fiona — she always stayed cool.

"What if their name isn't on the list?" Jenelle asked, taking a seat behind the table.

"Too bad," Fiona said.

"What should I do?" I asked.

Fiona pursed her lips. "Why don't you go open the gate?" she suggested.

Open the gate? I looked at the crowd of people standing on the street. A couple of them had started up a chant: "Fi-o-na!" *Clap, clap, clap!* "Fi-o-na!" *Clap, clap, clap!* Some of the kids looked annoyed. But most of them looked like those people you see on evening news shows the week before Christmas — like they couldn't wait to get in and grab everything they could. I gulped.

Still, I didn't have much of a choice. I took a few deep breaths — like my mom is always doing when Kirk accidentally sticks silverware in the garbage disposal — and made my way to the gate. The chanting started in earnest as I lifted the latch. With the force of a tidal wave, the crowd burst through the gates, throwing me backward. I landed on my butt, crushing a lovely bed of black-eyed Susans and dahlias.

"I'm fine!" I shouted as my schoolmates streamed past me. "No problem — just ruined my new outfit, but I'm good."

Nobody even glanced in my direction as I hauled myself to my feet and brushed the bark off. They just shot forward, trampling the pristine grass, desperate for their invitations.

Fiona stood behind the table, watching the scene with folded arms. Cool as an iceberg.

I wondered what it would be like to care so little about what other people thought of you.

*   *   *

By the time Jake dropped me off at my house, my legs were stiff and sore. After I'd opened the gates, Fiona had asked me to hand out lemonade to people in the line. That meant endless trips running up and down the marble stairs, passing out glasses and collecting empty cups. But I'd gotten what I wanted — the DVD invitation was tucked safely into my flowered bag. And Fiona had even smiled at me when she handed it over. "Thanks," she'd said. "I'm really glad you were here."

I had just taken a sip of lemonade when she said that, and almost choked in surprise. Luckily, Fiona had already walked off to talk to some girl with pale blond hair and nearly invisible eyebrows. Her name wasn't on the list, and she was pitching an absolute fit. Not that Fiona cared. She just wanted the girl to leave.

"Hey," I said as I walked into the kitchen. Everyone in my family uses the back door. I'm not really sure why.

"Hi, sweetie," Mom said. She was sitting at the table, chopping carrots into tiny matchsticks. "Do you want to help me cut up some stuff for your dad?"

"Sure," I said. "But can I call Elise quickly?" She and I had a date to talk over my first day at Allington.

"Of course." Mom's mouth twisted as she concentrated on slicing the carrots. I know I shouldn't say this about my own mother, but she isn't a very good cook. I mean, she can hardly boil water or slice a cucumber. Like, right now, all of her carrots were uneven and different sizes. But it's nice that she tries to help.

I pulled the science magnet from my bag and stuck it on the refrigerator, then yanked the cordless phone off the wall and dialed. It rang four times, then the voice mail came on. *Weird*, I thought. I left a message and sat down to help my mom. But I felt like an old volleyball — half deflated and a little scuffed. I'd wanted to tell Elise all about Jenelle and Fiona and my sandwich and the party. . . .

"How was school?" she asked. "Did you have fun with Jenelle?"

I decided to spare Mom the details. I love my mom and all, but it was really Elise I wanted to talk to just then. "I've been invited to a party," I told her.

"Oh, that's wonderful, honey!" Mom said, her face radiant. Like getting invited to a party on your first day of school was a huge triumph. Which it kind of was, come to think of it. "What are you going to wear?"

"I'm not sure," I admitted. "I think it's formal. I'll have to check the invitation."

Mom put down her knife and ran her fingers through her long ponytail. "Do you have it? Let me look at it."

"Actually — it's a DVD," I admitted. "I'll have to watch it later."

"A DVD?" A slight frown formed at the edges of my mother's eyes. "Isn't that wasteful?"

"Well . . ." See, my mom works for an environmental nonprofit, managing their fund-raisers and organizing all of their events. She's really into the environment. When I was younger, I used to tell people that her favorite hobby was finding ways to save water. ". . . I think the idea is that the DVD is a keepsake," I said. "It's not like a paper invitation, which just wastes trees and goes in the recycling."

"Hmm." Mom looked dubious, but she didn't say anything else. She had her doubts about the party already, I could tell.

After dinner, we walked over to our favorite ice-cream place — True Moo — for dessert. I checked the voice mail when we got back, but Elise still hadn't called, so I finished up my magnet experiments.

Finally, as I was typing up my notes on the computer, an IM flashed in the corner of my screen. It was Elise.

Blakesgrl: U there?

Ugh, I thought. *When did she change her screen name? Blake's girl? Shudder.*

Flwrpwr: Hey. Forget our date?
Blakesgrl: Sorry! Started talking to Blake and lost trk of time. Four hrs!!

My fingers paused at the edge of the keyboard. Elise forgot about me because she was talking to *Blake*? My stomach felt like an empty space in the center of my body. I didn't know how to respond.

After a moment, another message blinked onto the screen.

Blakesgrl: Really sorry

I stared at the cursor, watching it appear and disappear, appear and disappear, waiting for my reply. I was angry, sure. Then again, maybe I was

overreacting. Elise had said that she was sorry. . . .
And we'd been friends a long time.

Flwrpwr: It's okay
Blakesgrl: Can u talk now?

I checked the clock in the corner of my screen. It was eight ten. My parents really don't like for me to be on the phone after eight, but I was sure they would make an exception this once, since it was my first day and all. But, suddenly, I really didn't feel like chatting with Elise. I just wasn't in the mood.

Flwrpwr: Maybe tomorrow?
Blakesgrl: Want to hang? Daily Blend?

Daily Blend was our favorite smoothie place-slash-coffee bar. It had old, plush couches and shelves full of books that people used as a local library. Plus, they had the best raspberry smoothies in town.

Flwrpwr: Definitely.
Blakesgrl: C U then!
Flwrpwr: Bye.

I finished up my homework and then went upstairs to get ready for bed. It was early, but I was tired. As I was changing into my favorite soft pajamas with the blue sky and fluffy clouds on them, Pizza came in and looked up at my bed hopefully. The hardwood floor in my bedroom is a little slippery, and it makes it hard for Pizza to get onto the bed.

"You want to get up, sweetie?" I asked her. Gently, I lifted my old lady dog onto the foot of my bed, where she immediately curled into a puffball and went to sleep. *She looks like a dandelion,* I thought as I ran my hand over her soft fur. I remembered when we got Pizza. She was three years old and still full of crazy energy — always chasing her tail or darting after dust balls or begging to play fetch with her favorite fabric Frisbee. Now that she's eleven, she doesn't run around much anymore. She mostly likes to cuddle on the couch. *But that's okay,* I thought as I raked my fingers through the long fur on her ears. Pizza looked up at me with sleepy brown eyes, then gave the back of my hand a lick. I leaned over, putting my face beside hers and breathing in her warm doggie smell.

As I settled back into bed and closed my eyes I thought, *It's nice to know that there's at least one person in the world who will love you no matter what.*

CHAPTER FOUR

League Rule #4:
When you're out, you're out.

"I can*not* believe this is happening," Fiona huffed as she dropped dramatically into the chair behind mine the next morning.

"It's such a joke?" Lucia agreed, grabbing the seat behind Fiona's. "It's, like, so completely unfair?"

"What's going on?" I asked as Jenelle slipped into the desk beside me. I was trying to play it cool — even though I was more than a little shocked that the League had decided to sit with me today. I couldn't help noticing that the rest of the class was shooting glances in our direction, and I heard this one girl with crazy curly black hair say, "Who's the new girl?" Wow. Five seconds with the League, and I'd solved my invisibility problem.

Fiona's blue eyes narrowed. "Some dumb parents found out about my party."

"They're complaining because their kids weren't invited," Jenelle explained. She was wearing her blond hair in a sleek ponytail today, with a piece of hair hiding the elastic. She had on a short green dress and green shoes, and looked elegant. Even though I had on a dress, too — a sleeveless shift with tomatoes printed on it — I still felt a little sloppy-looking compared to the League.

I'd spent half an hour blow-drying my hair, but the minute I stepped outside, the humidity had made it frizz out. Plus, I'd tripped walking up to the steps to the school, scuffing the front of my right shoe. I tucked my right foot behind my left self-consciously as Fiona added, "They reported me to Headmistress Cardinal, and she called my parents to 'gently suggest' that I ruin my party."

"She wants you to cancel?" I asked.

Fiona scoffed. "Worse," she said, pursing her lips as if she had just taken a big swig of vinegar.

"The school wants Fiona to, like, invite everyone?" Lucia supplied, rolling her large brown eyes. She was wearing a brown halter top and matching skirt, and the color made her eyes look even choc-olatier than usual. She fiddled with the tassel on her Stuart Weitzman wristlet bag.

"Everyone?" I repeated.

Jenelle nodded. "The whole seventh and eighth grades."

"The parents don't want their little mini-morons to feel bad," Fiona snapped. "Just because they're losers."

"Can't you just say no?" I asked, even though I didn't see the problem with inviting everyone in the seventh and eighth grades. Personally, I thought it sounded like even more fun.

"I tried, but my mother is terrified of the head-mistress." Fiona snorted in disgust. "She gave in right away."

Just then, two boys darted through the class-room door, and an instant later, the bell rang. The teacher, Ms. Albermarle, got up from her desk to shut the door after them. Her policy is that people who are late don't get into the class. She makes them go the principal's office. *What is it about math teachers that makes them so much stricter than anyone else?* I wondered as she walked toward the door.

Jenelle cast a glance at Fiona. I saw their eyes meet for a moment, and then Jenelle reached into

80

her purse. "Hey, Amy," she said, as she handed me a plastic bottle of Diet Coke. "Here."

The bottle had just started to get slippery with condensation, making my hand slightly damp as I took it. "Um, thanks," I said, slightly confused. I mean, I drink Diet Coke sometimes . . . but it seemed kind of like a weird present.

Jenelle jerked her chin toward the front of the class, where Ms. Albermarle was shaking her head at a scrawny boy on the other side of the door who was begging through the glass window to be let in. Ms. Albermarle, by the way, is a dead ringer for the queen in Disney's *Alice in Wonderland* movie. You know, if the queen wore ugly pantsuits instead of being dressed like a playing card. "It's for her," Jenelle whispered. "She's addicted to it."

Fiona leaned forward to hiss in my ear. "We had her last year," she said. "Trust me, give her the drink. It's a guaranteed extra five points on the midterm."

"Oh," I said as my heart tripped over itself. *Jeez,* I thought, *is this my lucky day or what?* For one thing, Fiona seemed to have seriously chilled out since the day before. I guess helping her with her party really paid off. *And now, the League is letting me in on Secret Albermarle Extra Credit!*

Flashing Jenelle a grateful smile, I hauled myself out of my desk and hurried to the front of the class.

My plan had been to just leave the drink at the edge of her desk, but Ms. Albermarle turned away from the door at just that second. "What's this?" she demanded, scowling.

"Um — apple for the teacher?" I joked, holding out the drink.

Light laughter rippled through the class, but Albermarle's scowl lifted, like a passing rain cloud. "Ah," she said, reaching for the drink. "Just what I *needed*. Thank you so much, Ms. Flowers."

Relief flooded my system, and I turned to grin at Jenelle just as Ms. Albermarle twisted the cap off of the soda. Instantly, the drink *exploded,* spouting dark, sticky liquid everywhere. I swear, I once saw a geyser go off, and this was worse than Old Faithful. The drink splattered me in the face, and it completely drenched the front of Ms. Albermarle's hideous yellow suit. She spluttered as droplets collected in her hair, dousing her face and smearing her makeup.

Finally, finally, the drink hissed and calmed down, and the two of us were left standing there in a puddle of soda, staring at each other, as the class cracked up. Ms. Albermarle's eyes widened until I thought they were going to pop out of her head. Her smudged makeup made her look even more terrifying than usual as she turned to the class and bellowed, "Silence!"

I cringed as she turned back to me. I moved my lips to say, "I didn't mean to!" but I couldn't force a sound out of my mouth. I just made this weird choking-gasping sound that came out like "Eaucch."

Albermarle pointed to the door. "Headmistress," she hissed, forcing the word through clenched teeth. I raced to my desk for my books and my bag and beat it out of there like a bullet.

I didn't even breathe until I reached the end of the hall. When I turned the corner, I paused to take a shaky breath. *What just happened?* I wondered as hot tears formed behind my eyelids. But the answer was obvious — the bottle had gotten shaken up while Jenelle was carrying it around in her bag. *I'll just tell Headmistress Cardinal it was an accident,* I reasoned as I slowly began walking toward the administrative office. The thought made me feel a little better. *After all,* I *got seriously sprayed, too,* I realized. She'll have to believe it was an accident. And I'll apologize to Ms.

Albermarle later. *Besides,* I thought, *look at the bright side . . . .*

At least she didn't say, "Off with her head."

"Not horrible," I said as I tossed a damp paper towel into the wastepaper basket. I'd hurried to the girls' room to try to repair some of the Diet Coke damage. It wasn't easy. The biggest problem was my hair. It was a sticky, frizzy mess. But I'd run some water through it and found an elastic at the bottom of my bag to tie it back, so it was more or less under control.

There wasn't much I could do about my outfit. Unfortunately, my dress was white with red tomatoes on it, and the top half really showed the cola-colored splatters. I stared at myself in the mirror for a moment, taking in my reflection — straight nose that's just a little too long, green eyes that are a little too wide apart, pointy chin with a scar on the lower right from when I fell off my bicycle when I was seven. I'm not gorgeous like Lucia and Fiona — or even super-pretty, like Jenelle. But I'm not ugly either. I like to think that my face has character. "Time to face the music," I said aloud. Then I pulled in a deep breath and pushed my way through the rest-room door.

I was just about to walk into the administrative office when Scott walked out. "Hey!" he said brightly, giving me a smile.

"Hi . . ." I could feel my pulse pumping through my entire body, but I still couldn't manage much of a smile.

"What's wrong?" he asked. "You okay?"

I gestured to my outfit. "There was . . . an accident," I explained. "Involving an exploding soda and Ms. Albermarle."

Scott's face went white. "Albermarle . . ." He groaned. "Oh, *no*." Then he gave a little snort that sounded almost like a laugh. "Did she get —"

"Completely sprayed? Yes. Her yellow pantsuit has a definite brown splotchy giraffe-pattern now."

Scott actually did laugh then, and even I managed a giggle. "Oh, I wish I could have seen her face," he said.

"Yeah, me too," I agreed. "But I was too busy watching my life as it passed before my eyes." He grinned, and I felt myself relax a little. Which was practically a miracle, given the circumstances. I've only ever been called to the principal's office once, and that was in order to participate in the final round of the fifth grade spelling bee. I lost on "obstreperous." Anyway.

"I have to see the headmistress," I told Scott. "What are you doing here?" I allowed myself a moment of hope that maybe he'd gotten in trouble, too, and would tell me that it wasn't so bad, Headmistress Cardinal is a softie, blah, blah, blah. . . .

But no such luck. "Nothing exciting," he admitted, holding up a hall pass. "I had a dentist appointment."

"I just wish I didn't look like such a disaster," I admitted, glancing down at my ruined dress.

"Really?" Scott cocked his head as if he didn't think I looked so bad. "Here." He peeled off his black zip-front hoodie and handed it to me. "You can borrow this."

It was still warm, and smelled like him — like a mixture of soap and fabric softener. The weight of it in my hand was enough to make me feel a little woozy. *I'm holding Scott Lawton's hoodie,* I thought. *Just thirty seconds ago, he was wearing this!* "Are you sure?" I asked.

"Just don't spill Pepsi all over it," he joked. "Or toss it in the wash if you do. Hey, I'll see you later, okay?" With a quick smile, he jogged off.

"Thanks!" I called after him. "I'll be careful with this!" I added, holding up the hoodie.

You sound like an idiot, the smart part of my brain told my mouth. But Scott didn't seem to mind. He just waved over his shoulder, then disappeared behind a bank of lockers.

I pulled on the sweater and zipped up the front. Perfect. The bottom half of my dress was untouched by soda, and my shoes and bag were black. I even kind-of-almost-but-not-really matched. Plus, have I mentioned that this sweatshirt belonged to the cutest boy at Allington Academy, not to mention the known universe?

"Hello, derlin'!" The school receptionist had huge blond hair, bright pink lipstick, and the thickest Texas accent I've ever heard. The plaque at the front of her desk said her name was Kathy Snell. "Well, aren't you just the cutest thang — look at that derlin' skirt! If I was twenty years younger and twenty sizes smaller, I'd be all over that like white on rice!"

"Um . . . thank you," I said. "Er . . . I'm here to see Headmistress Cardinal."

"Uh-oh!" Kathy lifted her drawn-on eyebrows playfully. "What did you *do*?" She leaned forward to rest her chin in her hands, listening eagerly.

"I accidentally sprayed Ms. Albermarle with a Coke." I winced.

"Oooh!" Kathy's cheeks puffed out. "You're in trouble now, ain'tcha?" She winked at me, as if being in trouble was the most fun thing in the world. "And you picked the worst possible day!" she said brightly, picking up a pencil and the phone receiver. "The headmistress is out of the office all day long at a conference. So you'll have to see Mr. Denton, the dean of students. Mm-*mm*." Shaking her head, she dialed a four-digit extension using the pencil's eraser. "Hello, sir. I'm afraid we've got a rabble-rouser out here to see ya. Yep. Okay!" She smiled brightly and hung up the phone. "Just have a seat," she said cheerfully. "He'll be right with you."

I dropped onto one of the plush leather chairs that were arranged along the wall and settled in to wait. After ten minutes, the bell rang to start a new period. *Great,* I thought. *Now I'm missing lunch.*

Apparently, Kathy had a different understanding of the phrase "be right with you" than the one I was used to, because I sat there for a full forty-seven minutes before a tall, bald man with a mustache appeared before me. He wore a long-sleeved blue shirt and a striped tie, but no jacket. "Ms. Flowers?" he asked.

"Yes," I told him, standing up.

"Yes?" he repeated. Planting his hands on his hips, Mr. Denton cocked his head and looked at me as if he wasn't sure what to make of me.

I tried again. "Um . . . yes, that's me."

Mr. Denton folded his arms across his broad chest. His forearms were like two giant hams. "It seems to me that sentence is missing something."

Missing something? I thought. *Does he want me to say the punctuation out loud?* I seriously wasn't getting it, so I sneaked a glance at Kathy, who mouthed, *sir.* "Oh!" I said to Mr. Denton. "Yes, sir, I'm Amy Flowers."

Kathy looked from me to Mr. Denton and shook her head, chuckling softly.

"Come with me, Ms. Flowers." The dean of students turned on his heel and strode out the door. His office was across the hall. It was very nice: The walls were lined with shelves full of books and trophies, and it was decorated with the same soft leather chairs they had in the main office. "I coach lacrosse and soccer," Mr. Denton explained when he caught me looking at a large silver trophy. He gestured toward one of the large leather chairs. "Please sit down."

I took a seat as he settled behind his desk. He picked up a pen and clicked it ten times, glaring at me the whole time. I have to admit that the combination of the clicking and the stare made me kind of nervous. I wasn't sure if I should speak or not. Finally, I decided that somebody had to say something, so I cleared my throat.

"Ms. Albermarle has already explained the situation to me," Mr. Denton said, clicking the pen a final time and leaning back in his chair. "That was a very cruel prank you pulled, young lady."

"Sir, I didn't mean —"

"You've upset a teacher with a twenty-four-year record of excellent service to this school," Mr. Denton went on, ignoring me. "And I hope that you're prepared to pay the price for it."

I swallowed hard. "Honestly, sir, I had no idea —"

"Don't tell me you had no idea!" Mr. Denton brought his palm down on his desk, which made the silver-framed photos that sat at the edge rattle. "That's what is wrong with America! You've got to face the music, Ms. Flowers!" Leaning forward, he clicked his pen five times and scribbled something on a yellow legal pad. "One week of after-school detention," he announced.

I felt my face burning. "But — but don't you want to hear —"

He didn't look up from his legal pad. "We're

done here. Ms. Snell will give you a pass to your next class."

I sat there for a moment, completely stunned. After waiting almost an hour, our conversation had lasted less than three minutes. *Don't say it's not fair,* I commanded myself, even though it *wasn't* fair — it was *completely* unfair! I hadn't even had a chance to say a single thing. *And don't you start,* I commanded my cheeks, which were already on fire with anger. I felt my throat tightening, and my chest felt like a python had wrapped itself around me and was starting to squeeze. . . .

My legs were weak, but I forced myself to stand and walk out of his office. Once outside in the main hall, I took a few deep breaths and blinked hard to get rid of the tears that had collected behind my eyes.

"Well, looks like you survived!" Kathy said as I walked back into the reception area.

"Barely," I told her.

"Mmm." Kathy pursed her lips and nodded knowingly. "Yes, Mr. Denton can be the chairman of the disapproval committee sometimes, don't I know it!" She giggled as she handed me a hall pass. "What did he give you? Five years of hard labor?"

"A week of detention," I admitted. I winced, imagining how I would explain the punishment to my mom.

"Just a week? Well, honey, he must like you!" Kathy smiled sweetly. "I swear, I've seen him give a month for a third-time gum-chewing infraction. Now git on to your next class." She flicked her long fingernails at me.

I looked up at the clock over the door. I'd missed science completely . . . so now it was on to Spanish. I sighed. *Oh, well,* I thought. *I guess Kathy has a point — it could be worse.*

Not that I expected my parents to understand that.

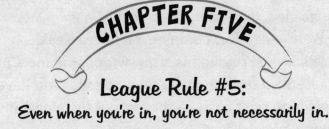

CHAPTER FIVE

League Rule #5:
Even when you're in, you're not necessarily in.

"Hi, Elise?" I cupped my hand around the phone receiver as students stood at their lockers nearby, slamming doors or shuffling through books. The last bell had just rung, and I had exactly seven minutes before I had to get to detention. I was huddled in a corner at the end of the science wing, standing at Allington Academy's one and only pay phone. The top of the phone was actually dusty . . . which I think proves my point — that everyone in the universe has a cell phone except me. "Listen, are you at Daily Blend?" I could hear the guilt in my own voice. Langton Middle School gets out fifteen minutes before Allington, so I figured that Elise was already there, waiting for me.

"Amy? Hey! Yeah, we're here! Where are you?" She giggled, then said, "Stop that!"

Wait — *we*? But I didn't even have to ask.

"Blake just tossed his straw wrapper at me. Cut it out!" She laughed again, then added, "You have to get here right away — they've got the pineapple coconut special!"

I groaned. The pineapple coconut smoothie was my absolute favorite — and they only had it about once a month. "That's just it — I can't make it," I confessed. "I've got detention."

"What?" she squealed. "Omigosh, what happened? Wait, hold on —" Elise's voice got softer, as if she had pulled the phone away from her ear. "Yes, she's fine. She's got detention. Okay." She must have put the phone back up to her mouth, because suddenly her voice was trumpeting in my ear. "Blake says that's dreads."

"Dreads?" I asked.

"Oh, sorry. That's just this thing Blake and I say. Dreads, like, it's *dreadful*."

Great. So now my best friend and her boyfriend were making up a secret language. I felt like I was having this conversation with someone from a distant planet.

"Hey! There's Jolina and Jules! Do you want to say hi?" Elise asked. "Hey, guys!" she called. "Over here."

"I can't." My stomach sank at the image of my friends — Jolina, who always wore her hair in a braid that ran down her entire back, and Jules, who was round and cheerful and had a mass of curly red hair — sitting down with Elise and Blake. I pictured them all laughing and drinking pineapple coconut smoothies . . . without me. "I've really got to get to detention."

"Okay, well, call me later!" Elise chirped. "Bye!"

"Bye," I said as she clicked off. I hung the receiver back in its place, slowly. *She didn't even ask me why I had detention,* I realized as I turned and trudged toward Mr. Denton's office. *I guess she figured that I'd tell her all of the details later. Maybe she thought I didn't have time to go into it now.*

Or maybe she just really doesn't care.

Don't think that, I told myself firmly as I knocked softly on Mr. Denton's dark brown oak door. It was slightly ajar, and when he said, "You may step forward," I pushed it open and walked in.

Mr. Denton was there, standing behind his desk with his back toward me, facing the large window that framed a scene of the quadrangle.

Students were seated beneath leafy trees, already working on homework. Beyond them, a group of boys were kicking a soccer ball back and forth on the playing fields. "You may have a seat, Ms. Flowers," Mr. Denton said, not looking at me.

I sat down in the plush chair, which sighed under my weight. Mr. Denton just stood there, and I wondered if we would spend the entire ninety minutes with me sitting in the chair and him staring out the window when someone shoved the door open wide and barged into the office.

"Am I late?" Mitchie asked. Her eyebrows flew up when she saw me. "Hey!"

Mr. Denton turned toward us. He stroked his mustache thoughtfully, then checked his watch. "You have forty seconds to spare, Ms. Ohara," he informed her.

"Gorgeous!" she said, flopping into the seat beside mine.

Mr. Denton scowled at her.

"I mean, 'Gorgeous, sir!'" Mitchie corrected herself.

Mr. Denton's mouth pinched into a frown. "Don't get too comfortable," he told us. He started toward the door, gesturing for us to follow. "Athletic team tryouts are next week," he said as he led us through the hall and down the front steps. "I have a lot to do to prepare for the season, and I don't have time to babysit you two." He led us to the fountain, where a stout man in a green jumpsuit stood. He wore thick glasses that made his eyes look enormous, and he was beaming at us. "So I've arranged for you to help Gerardo, here." Mr. Denton turned to Gerardo. "They're all yours," he announced, before stalking off.

Gerardo watched him for a moment. Once the dean of students was out of sight, he turned to us. "Mitchie," he said, making a disapproving clucking sound with his tongue. He had a slight Mexican accent that made her name sound more like "Meetchee." "What have you done now?"

"I got caught riding my skateboard on the library steps," Mitchie admitted.

Gerardo huffed like he wasn't surprised. "I don't think I know you," he said, eyeing me.

"I'm Amy," I told him.

"Well, it is a pleasure to meet you, Amy," Gerardo said with a smile. "Now girls, what we need to do is just a little weeding among these flower beds, here." He gestured to the colorful blooms against the stone wall that wrapped around the front of the school. He handed each of us a tool that looked kind of like the long fork my dad uses when he barbecues something.

"What's this?" I asked.

"It's a dandelion fork," Gerardo explained. "When you see a weed, you need to dig it out, pull it up by the roots. Otherwise, the weed will just come back." He took a deep breath and looked up at the sky. "It's a perfect day to work with the plants, yes? You girls are very lucky. Very, very lucky. Okay!" He rubbed his hands together. "I will go and get some mulch, and when I come back, you will have pulled a nice pile of weeds." With a nod, Gerardo turned and hurried off.

Mitchie and I just stood there for a moment, looking at each other. Shouts sounded from the playing fields. A clump of sixth-grade girls glanced at us as they hurried through the courtyard. One of them pointed at me and whispered something to her friends, then they all giggled.

"So," I said finally. "This doesn't seem so bad."

"It's not." Mitchie started toward the beds. She knelt down near a bright yellow flower and dug at a scraggly-looking plant that had sprouted nearby. "Gerardo is great. It's when Denton sticks you with laundry duty that you should start to worry." She shuddered a little as she pulled up the weed.

"What's wrong with laundry?" I asked, kneeling a few feet away from her. The flower bed had looked pristine from a distance. But up close, I could see the small weeds starting to form. I pulled at a clump of clover, and it came out easily.

Mitchie turned her sharp black eyes on me. "It's like working on the surface of the sun," she said. "It's so hot, it'll practically melt your face off. And you have to deal with stinky athletic uniforms. Believe me, the smell would choke a roach."

"Gross," I said.

"Besides, Mrs. Bagell is totally nuts," Mitchie went on, stabbing at a weed. "She makes you listen as she sits there reading tabloid articles about aliens abducting people and bat boys being found in caves."

"Why do I get the feeling that you've had a lot of detention?" I asked.

Mitchie just laughed. "I'm not supposed to ride my skateboard on the library steps . . . but sometimes, it's just too tempting. So, what did you do?"

I told her about spraying Ms. Albermarle.

Mitchie shifted her weight off of her knees, sitting down to face me. She watched me dig in the dirt for a while. Her short black hair was gleaming in the sun. Finally, she asked, "Who told you to give her a Diet Coke?"

"Jenelle told me she's addicted," I admitted.

"So," Mitchie said slowly, "you went and bought some and gave it to Ms. Albermarle?"

"No — Jenelle had the soda already," I explained. "I think it must have gotten shaken up in her purse."

Mitch's only comment was, "Hmm."

Something about that little grunt made me look at her, but she had turned back to her weeding. Just then Gerardo came bouncing up to us in a golf cart. The rear was loaded with plastic sacks of mulch.

"I'm back!" he sang cheerfully. "And I have the cedar mulch! Oh, it smells wonderful! You girls are gonna love it! Now you help me unload." He climbed out from behind the driver's wheel and danced to the back of the cart, as if he couldn't wait to get his hands on that mulch.

I had to shake out my stiff legs as I stood to help. The bags were really heavy — Gerardo could lift two at a time easily, but Mitchie and I had to work together to move just one.

Well, there's one thing about gardening, I thought as Mitchie and I hauled a bag to the section we had finished weeding. *I'm getting plenty of exercise.*

And at least as long as I'm in detention, I added mentally, *I don't have to face my parents.*

*   *   *

I wonder how long it will take Mom to mention detention, I thought as I walked into the dining room. Kirk was already helping himself to a piece of Mexican chicken mole — I guessed Dad finally moved on from his Asian-cooking kick — and Mom was filling the water glasses.

"Amy, there you are," Dad said as he backed through the swinging door that led to the kitchen, a bowl of steaming corn in his hands. "I haven't seen you all afternoon."

"Amy had detention today." Mom flipped her napkin into her lap, all business.

Kirk made a little choking noise and gaped at me with bug eyes.

"What?" Dad sat down, looking a little stunned. "What happened?"

"It was a total accident," I said quickly.

"Why don't you tell us what happened?" Mom suggested.

So, for what felt like the zillionth time, I explained about the Diet Coke and Ms. Albermarle. "But I had no idea that it was going to explode like that," I insisted.

"Hoo, that's *classic,*" Kirk said, shaking his head.

Mom glared at him.

"What?" Kirk picked up his ear of corn and

gestured with it, like a fat conductor's wand. "Little Miss Never-Gets-in-Trouble has detention on her second day of class? Awesome!" He made a face at me, chuckling, then took a big, crunchy bite of his corn.

Mom and Dad exchanged a sideways look. Finally, Dad pushed his glasses up on his nose and cleared his throat. "Amy, you're on a scholarship —"

"I know —"

Mom leaned forward to point her fork at me. "Which the school could choose to revoke at any time," she finished for him.

I sighed. "I *know*," I said quietly. I picked at the small piece of chicken on my plate. Chicken mole is usually my favorite, but tonight I didn't have much of an appetite.

For a moment, everyone was silent. The only sound was of silverware against plates and Kirk's noisy chewing. After a few minutes, he chuckled again, then took another huge bite of mole. "Classic," he muttered. It was very tempting to toss my chicken at his head, but I restrained myself.

"So, are you going to punish me?" I asked at last.

"Yes," Kirk mumbled.

"Do you think we need to?" Mom sat back in her chair and reached for her water glass.

"Not really," I said honestly. "I mean, it really was an accident. And I've already got to serve a week of detention for it."

Dad put his elbows on either side of his plate and pressed his fingertips together. "I think that's punishment enough," he said.

"Ernest," Mom said, gesturing toward his elbows. He quickly picked them off the table.

"What?" Kirk cried. "Are you serious? If *I'd* gotten detention, I'd have been grounded for a week!"

"If you'd gotten detention, it would have been because you hijacked the school's PA system to announce that the belching squad had a meeting at three PM," I shot back.

Kirk grinned. "Yeah, that was funny," he said. He had a corn kernel stuck between his front teeth, but I didn't say anything. *I hope it stays there until tomorrow, and that he grins at every single teacher and crush he's ever had in his life.*

"May I be excused?" I asked. "I'm really not hungry."

Mom's mouth twisted sympathetically. I could tell that she believed that the soda incident was an accident. "Okay, sweetheart," she said.

I took my plate to the kitchen and then headed up the back stairs to my room. I flopped on my bed and picked up the book I was supposed to be reading for English. It was called *To Kill A Mockingbird,* and it was good — I'd already read the first three chapters. But I was having trouble concentrating. I kept reading the same page over and over . . . and I still couldn't remember what happened. Finally, I gave up. Just as I slipped the book back into my bag, the phone rang.

"Hello?" I said, settling against my enormous pile of pink and orange pillows.

"Amy? It's Fiona."

For a moment, I was too surprised to respond.

"Hello? Are you there?"

"Yes, sorry — I was just —" Just what? Too freaked out by your voice to speak? "What's going on?" I asked.

"I just wanted to let you know that I heard you got detention," she said. "Jenelle feels really awful. She didn't know that the soda was going to detonate."

"I know," I told her.

"She was really upset all day," Fiona went on. "She wanted to tell Ms. Albermarle that it was her fault, but I talked her out of it. I mean,

104

what is the point of everyone getting in trouble, right?"

I thought about that. It was nice that Jenelle wanted to defend me. And Fiona *did* have a point. "Right," I said.

"Anyway, she had to go to this reception with her mother tonight, so she asked me to call you to apologize. And to give you the science assignment."

Wow, I thought. *That's actually* nice *of her.* Maybe Jenelle was right — maybe Fiona really could be a good friend once you got to know her. "Answer the questions on page twelve, right?" I said. I'd seen Anderson in the hall right before last period.

"Not that," Fiona corrected. "The extra-credit assignment."

"Extra credit?" I repeated. Anderson hadn't mentioned it. *Then again,* I reasoned, *Anderson doesn't exactly seem like the extra-credit type.* "What is it?"

"Apparently tomorrow is National Science Day." Fiona gave a little snort. "Mr. Pearl said that anyone who dresses up in a science-related costume will get ten extra-credit points on the next exam."

"Are you actually going to do that?" I asked. Somehow, I couldn't imagine Fiona dressed as the solar system or a lab rat or whatever.

"Well . . . I've got this gold shirt left over from that metallic fad last year," she admitted. "Gold's on the periodic table of the elements, so I figured, why not? I've got a gold purse, too, and matching shoes."

Leave it to Fiona to turn a science costume into a fashion project.

"Jenelle's going as platinum, and Lucia thinks she can pull off copper. But Pearlie said anything science-related is fine."

"What should I be?" I asked. I didn't really have any metallic clothes. Flower prints, yes . . .

"I don't know . . . lead?" she suggested.

"Actually, I think I've got an idea," I told her, sliding off my bed. I walked over to my closet and pulled out a green-and-yellow shirt. *Hmm,* I thought, *it might work.*

"What is it?" Fiona asked.

"You'll see tomorrow," I told her.

"I can't wait." Her voice sounded like she really meant it.

I hung up the phone and dug through my tights drawer, then pulled out my favorite boots and a skirt I'd bought at a yard sale the year before. *It's perfect,* I thought as I scanned the outfit. *Now all I need is the perfect hair.*

Mom's right, I thought as I hurried to the bathroom to see what I could scrounge up. *I have to be careful — I don't want to get kicked out of Allington. It's the coolest place in the world!*

CHAPTER SIX

League Rule #6:
You can't be weird and cool at the same time.

The minute I stepped off the bus in the morning, I had a bad feeling.

Okay, maybe I should have.been suspicious when the bus attendant looked at me like I'd just escaped from a prison for the criminally insane. And maybe I should have thought that something was up when nobody on the bus was in costume. But none of those kids were in my science class, so I didn't really worry about it.

But when I got to school, I started worrying.

A clump of eighth graders by the fountain stared at me as I walked into the courtyard. A tall girl with a short blond pixie cut snorted and whispered something to her friend.

Giggles and murmurs rippled around me as I walked toward the front steps, and I realized that everyone was staring at my clothes. And that was when I saw Rue Cotton. She had Mr. Pearl, too — she sat at the lab table across from mine. And she was wearing a blue-and-green plaid skirt and a blue shirt. So . . . unless she was dressed as some famous scientist with incredible fashion sense, she was definitely taking a pass on the extra credit.

Okay, okay, okay, I told myself as my heart hammered in my chest. *You know that Fiona's going to be dressed up, and the rest of the League will be, too.* . . . But when I walked by Jenelle's locker, she was wearing a yellow eyelet skirt and a white fitted halter. The minute she saw me, her mouth actually dropped open, and her eyes widened so far that I could see white all the way around them, like a fried egg. "Oh my . . ."

"Where's the silver?" I asked her, even though I had a bad feeling that I knew.

"Wh — what?" Her mouth snapped closed, and her eyelids drooped toward each other. "Silver?"

109

Suddenly, I heard a shriek of laughter behind us. I didn't even have to turn around to know that it was Fiona.

"Omigosh!" she cried as Lucia stood behind her, trying to stuff a guffaw back into her mouth with her manicured nails. "What are you supposed to *be*?"

I looked her up and down. She was wearing a pale blue brushed-cotton dress and had on green shoes with a blue flower pattern. No gold in sight — not even a bracelet. No costume.

I'd been set up.

I actually started to tremble then, I was so mad. But I didn't want her to know how angry I was. I wasn't about to give her the satisfaction. "I'm an amoeba," I told her. "And what are *you* supposed to be?" I asked. *The world's biggest experiment in jerkdom?* I added mentally.

Fiona eyed my green tights, green-and-yellow paisley shirt, and wild green-patterned skirt, cracking up. "What did you do to your *hair*?"

"It's semi-permanent," I told her. I'd had the color left over from Halloween two years before, when I dressed as a pineapple.

"It's *green*," she pointed out.

"Yeah, and it's like, a mile tall?" Lucia added.

"How long did you have to tease it? Like, five years?"

"What's going on?" Jenelle asked.

"Omigosh — you didn't *tell* her?" Lucia asked, dissolving into giggles again.

But I didn't wait to hear the rest of the conversation. I just turned and stalked off toward my locker, feeling completely and utterly amoeba-like.

"Don't say it," I said as I sat down next to Anderson. I'd been getting stares and comments all day long, and I was sick of it. I'd actually spent my lunch hour in the library, downing my sandwich as I walked down the hall. I wasn't about to sit with the League.

But Anderson couldn't help himself. "Crazy outfit," he said.

"Tell me about it," I mumbled. I heard whispering behind me, and knew that it was Fiona and Jenelle. Gritting my teeth, I flipped through the textbook, ignoring them.

"All right, all right, all right!" Mr. Pearl was carrying a large paper coffee cup in one hand and had his book in the other, so he had to shut the door with his elbow. "Let's get right to — whoa!

What's this we have here?" His huge frog eyes blinked at my outfit, and he smiled, as if he suspected that I was pulling a joke on the class. "Ms. Flowers, is there some explanation for this fashion choice?"

Titters rippled around me, and I heard Fiona give a little snort.

"I'm dressed up for National Science Day," I announced. "I'm an amoeba."

Mr. Pearl was so surprised that he actually dropped his science book and had to retrieve it. "It's a celebration of science!" he cried, placing the book on his desk and taking a long pull from his coffee cup. "Wonderful, wonderful! Ten extra-credit points on your next exam!"

"What?" Fiona growled behind me.

A murmur of protest ran through the room and I grinned. I really did get extra credit, after all!

Mr. Pearl typed a note on his laptop. "And, Mr. Sempe, what is your costume?" He looked at Anderson expectantly.

Anderson looked stunned. "Er —" He gaped at me for help.

"He's Louis Pasteur," I said quickly.

"Very clever!" Mr. Pearl boomed. "Of course, Pasteur pioneered germ theory — made sure that crazy green germs with wild hair and paisley skirts didn't attack us, eh? Ha-ha! Ten points for you as well, Mr. Sempe." His fingers flew across the keypad, recording the credit.

"Hey!" A guy at the front of the class named Preston Harringford protested. "Hey, I'm dressed up, too."

Mr. Pearl gave him a dubious look. "And who are *you* supposed to be, Mr. Harringford?"

Preston thought for a moment. "Um . . . Isaac Newton?"

"Where's your apple?" Mr. Pearl asked. "Nice try. No, no. Ms. Flowers and Mr. Sempe will be the only ones getting extra credit. Good for them!"

Anderson beamed at me. "You're a genius!" he whispered. Then he leaned toward me and added, "And your green hair looks great with your eyes." He flashed me a small smile, then turned back to his textbook as Mr. Pearl pulled down the screen for his PowerPoint presentation.

The smile made me feel warm — like a small spark of pride was glowing in my chest. I turned to sneak a peek at Fiona, but she was busy ignoring me, her lips in a tight line. But Jenelle was looking in my direction. Her hazel eyes flicked from me to Anderson, and then up to the screen, and I wondered if she'd overheard Anderson's compliment.

"Okay, people!" Mr. Pearl announced, turning back to face us. "First quiz is next Friday, so you'd better start studying. We'll cover all of chapter one, plus our first lab, which is next Wednesday. Remember people — be prepared!"

Anderson leaned toward me as Mr. Pearl launched into the day's lesson. "Hey, do you want to study together next Thursday, before the test?" he asked hopefully. "I could really use the help. . . ."

I hesitated. I knew Jenelle liked Anderson. Then again, we were just studying together, not going out. Besides, we were lab partners. We'd have to work together all year. "Sure," I told him. "Sounds good."

Anderson beamed. "Great," he said.

"Mr. Sempe, do you mind joining us?" Mr. Pearl asked from the front of the class. "I'm sure that whatever you have to say to Ms. Flowers can wait."

Anderson nodded, and we both turned back to our work. I even managed to smile a little. Thanks to Mr. Pearl and Anderson, this day hadn't been a total bust.

Maybe I'm not such an amoeba after all, I thought.

* * *

114

"This noise makes me feel like something is trying to claw its way up my back," Mitchie said as she scraped white paint from the iron fence.

"Yeah," I agreed as I scraped at my own section. "Something with tentacles."

"And huge teeth," Mitchie put in.

"And a burning desire to suck out my brain," I added.

Mitchie laughed. But, seriously, the metal-on-metal scraping sound was sending shivers up my spine. So far, today's detention was way worse than the day before. For one thing, gloriously groomed students *not* dressed as amoebas kept walking by, snickering at my outfit. For another, it was hot. We're talking hot — like toaster guts. And then there was the whole paint-scraping thing.

"You girls are doing great!" Gerardo said, coming up behind us. "Good job! When you finish, I can paint, and it will be perfect!" He beamed at us for a moment, then hurried off to trim the large box hedges at the front of the school. At least, I hope that's what he was doing with that huge electric buzz saw–looking thing.

"Don't look now," Mitchie said as I turned back to my scraping. "Someone over there keeps giving you the eye." She was peering out at the field in front of us, which a group of guys was using for an informal game of lacrosse. "He's a cutie, too."

I blew out a sigh. Even though I directed my breath at my bangs, they didn't move — the heat had plastered them to my forehead. "Mitchie, I hate to break it to you," I told her. "But lots of people are giving me the eye — my hair is *green*."

"I don't know. . . ." Mitchie singsonged as a huge flake of white paint dropped at her feet. "Something tells me this isn't a green-hair look." Then she gave this little laugh, as if she knew something I didn't. It sounded like "Heh-heh-*heh*."

It was the laugh more than anything that made me look up, and when I did, my heart sort of wobbled and fell over. Scott was standing at the edge of the field. And he *was* looking in my direction.

When he saw me looking, he lifted his hand in a little half-wave.

"Ooooh!" Mitchie said playfully. "We *know* him!" She waved back, and before I had a chance to do anything, a blue ball flew across the field and knocked Scott smack in the side of the head.

Mitchie winced, and as we looked at each other, I caught myself wondering if the look on my face was as hilarious as the look on hers. I guess it was, because she burst out laughing. "Oops," she said.

"He seems okay," I said. Scott had darted back onto the field, rubbing the side of his head. But he wasn't looking in my direction anymore.

"So, who is that?" Mitchie knocked her scraper against the fence playfully, producing a series of low bell-like dongs.

"He's just this guy," I told her. "He loaned me a sweatshirt yesterday. He probably just wants it back." I had been trying to sound as nonchalant as possible. It didn't really work, though, because I let out this goofy little giggle at the end.

"Oh, he's *just this guy,*" Mitchie said knowingly. "I see." She smiled a little, but she didn't ask anything else.

Just then, I felt a tap on my shoulder.

Standing behind me was this gorgeous, tall girl with long blond hair and creamy skin. I was pretty sure I'd seen her before, maybe on the cover of something. You know, like *Beautiful People Weekly.* She was wearing a trendy plaid skirt with a yellow polo top and yellow fabric mules, and she looked like she'd never even *heard* of sweat. "Don't you hang out with Fiona?" the beautiful girl asked.

"Um . . ." I wasn't really sure how to answer this question, so I did it Lucia-style. "Yes?"

"Cool." The girl flipped a hunk of gleaming hair over her shoulder. "I was just wondering how you got your hair so green."

For a moment, I thought she might be teasing me. But she looked really interested. "It's just this semi-permanent stuff, Wild Tangles. You can get it at Fabio's Hair Emporium."

The beautiful girl pulled a small notebook out of her handbag (plaid, to match her skirt) and wrote that down. "Cool," she said. "Well, thanks!" And then she walked away, her hair bouncing behind her.

"Hmm, now Voe Silk is interested in your hair." Mitchie rubbed her chin thoughtfully. "You sure are making an impression, Amy Flowers. She's queen dramarama of the eighth grade."

"She doesn't look like a dramarama," I said. At Langton, the drama kids had all been into heavy eyeliner and black clothes.

"She's going through a prep phase," Mitchie explained. "Before that, it was Goth. Before that, it was dancer-chic. She likes to mix it up. Maybe next she'll go for alien cool!" She gave me a sideways look and went back to scraping. "So, you haven't even told me what this outfit is all about, by the way."

"What makes you think it's about something?" I replied. "Maybe I just enjoy looking like E.T.'s cousin."

Mitchie laughed so hard that she nearly choked. "Okay, okay, don't tell me."

"No, it's okay," I said. "Yesterday, Fiona called and told me that today was National Science Day. She said the League was dressing up as elements from the periodic table — you know, silver, copper, platinum. She said that I'd get extra credit if I dressed up, too."

Mitchie gave a low whistle. "Man, she's good. Dressing as gold — it's just absurd enough to be believable."

I nodded. "That's what I thought."

"Well, she's probably done with you now, so you can breathe a sigh of relief."

I stopped what I was doing and turned to look at her carefully. "What do you mean?"

Mitchie set down her scraping tool. "Fiona loves to prank people. Like that shook-up Diet Coke thing? That's classic Fiona. She's pulled that on everyone." Mitchie shrugged. "Although having you pull it on Albermarle was a new twist," she admitted.

"But Jenelle gave me that drink," I pointed out.

"Yeah, that's why I didn't say anything yesterday." Mitchie tucked her glossy black hair behind an ear thoughtfully. "I thought it might be a coincidence. But she probably just handed the drink to Jenelle and made her give it to you. This amoeba outfit just proves it."

"I can't believe Jenelle would do that to me," I said, shaking my head.

Mitchie looked away. "It's hard to say no to Fiona." She seemed thoughtful for a moment. "Anyway, it's not so bad. She pulled a major prank on Lucia last year, just before she let her into the League."

"What did she do?" I asked, even though I wasn't sure I wanted to know the answer.

"Well, we were all on the school camping trip, and she waited until Lucia got into the shower. When Lucia had her eyes closed and her hair full of shampoo, Fiona started screaming that there was a snake in her stall. Lucia ran outside —"

"Oh my gosh!"

Mitchie nodded. "She had on a fluffy yellow towel, but that was it."

I felt myself blushing on Lucia's behalf. "That's so . . . mean."

"Mean?" Mitchie thought it over. "No, that's

just embarrassing. Fiona only gets mean when she really doesn't like you. Like, two years ago, she used to be good friends with this one girl. But she always made fun of the girl's super-long hair. The girl refused to cut it, and she and Fiona had a huge fight about it. So Fiona invited her to a slumber party at her house. Then, when the girl was asleep, Fiona hacked off her ponytail."

I gasped. That was the meanest thing I'd ever *heard* of. "And she got away with that?"

Mitchie drew her tool across the fence post, and light flakes of paint fluttered to the ground like snow. "She lost her friend over it," she said at last. "If that's what you mean." She turned and looked me square in the eye, and her gaze was so intense that I felt like she was looking right through me. "There are people who will tell you that Fiona can be the best friend you've ever had. Truly loyal. But if you ask me, I wouldn't trust her too much."

I nodded. From what I could tell, you could only count on Fiona to be loyal to one person — herself.

Later that night, I was just finishing up a one-page chapter summary for English class when a small white box appeared at the bottom of my computer screen.

jjjcutie: U there? it's jenelle.

   I watched the cursor blink on and off for a few moments, unsure how to respond. Or even whether to respond at all. *I could just turn this computer off right now,* I thought. But then another line appeared.

jjjcutie: I didn't know about today, I swear

   My pulse pounded in my ears and my fingers danced across the keyboard.

Flwrpwr: did u know about the coke?

   There was a long pause before the box popped up again.

jjjcutie: yes.
jjjcutie: and i'm really sorry. reallyreallyreally. but I thought it was the only way F would let u hang with us. she always pranks ppl in the beginning, then its over

I thought about that for a moment. I could still hear my heart in my ears, but the rhythm had slowed down a little. Okay, so Jenelle had played along with the first prank . . . but she didn't really do it to be mean. . . .

My computer dinged, and another message popped up.

jjjcutie: still there?
Flwrpwr: planning any more pranks?
jjjcutie: no. F's really happy. she saw you talking to Anderson. . . .

I rolled my eyes. *That's* so *Fiona,* I thought. *She's always happy when people are doing what she wants.* I typed a reply and hit SEND before I even had a chance to think.

Flwrpwr: I'm not even interested in Anderson

Once again, I had to wait a really long time before Jenelle replied. She must be typing a really long message, I thought, but when it popped up, all it said was:

jjjcutie: Really?

I smiled. Poor Jenelle. She really had a heart-stomping crush on Anderson.

Flwrpwr: Really . . . do u want me to find out if he's interested in someone else? ;-)
jjjcutie: No!
jjjcutie: Really, really, no, please. Promise you won't tell him that I like him!
Flwrpwr: I'd never do that, unless you told me to.
jjjcutie: Promise?
Flwrpwr: Promise.

She sounded so frantic that I actually giggled a little. *Maybe I can find out if Anderson is interested without giving Jenelle's crush away,* I thought. It was worth a shot. After all, Anderson wasn't exactly Sherlock Holmes. I could probably be subtle enough for him.

Just then, my mother stuck her head into my room. "Homework going okay?" she asked.

"I'm almost done," I told her.

She shoved her glasses higher onto her nose. "It's getting late." She leaned against my door frame, looking tired. Mom's been working on putting together an auction for her nonprofit, and I knew it was wearing her out.

"Ten minutes," I promised.

Mom nodded and moved on. Getting Kirk to shut off the computer is a forty-minute process, so she has to get started early. That's why I was so thrilled that Allington issued a laptop to every student. Before I had my own computer, I had to engage in some major Kirk-wrestling just to type up a little social studies.

I wrote a quick line to Jenelle.

Flwrpwr: I've gtg soon
jjjcutie: okay — quick. What are you doing sat? can u come to bounce? We need to find outfits for F's party.

Bounce? That was the store Jenelle's mother owned. I'd been dying to check it out. Plus, some Fiona-free hang time with Jenelle sounded excellent.

Flwrpwr: sounds great!
jjjcutie: c u there at 11?
Flwrpwr: perfect.
jjjcutie: kay. Bye.
Flwrpwr: bye.

I paused for a moment, letting the warm, happy feeling spread throughout my body. *Okay, so maybe the hard part is over,* I thought. No more pranks. And Jenelle wanted to get together. Plus, in a few days, I'd be at a super-cool party, hanging with my new friends.

All I had to do was figure out what to wear. I turned around in my chair and peered at my closet. I wondered if there was anything in there that would work. After all, Bounce was super-mondo-expensive — I couldn't possibly afford a whole outfit from there. *But maybe I could get some cool accessories,* I thought. *I could jazz up something I've already got. . . .*

I decided I'd better contact my fashion consultant. After all, I still had seven minutes left before I had to shut down, and Elise knew the clothes in my closet better than I did.

Flwrpwr: U there?

I could see from my buddy list that Elise was online . . . or at least her computer was on. But three minutes ticked away, and she didn't respond. Finally, I gave up. *She's probably chatting with Blake,* I reasoned, sighing.

It's a good thing Jenelle wants to get together, I thought. *Because it's starting to look like I may never see Elise again.*

CHAPTER SEVEN

League Rule #7:
The more something costs, the better it is.

"Sorry I'm late," I breathed as I rushed over to join Jenelle beside a rack of cool dresses in vibrant prints. "My dad agreed to drop my brother at his friend's house at the last minute, and —"

"Relax." Jenelle flashed me an amused smile. "You're only eight minutes late." She stood there, looking fresh and pretty in a red cotton dress that would have looked like a bag on me.

I was relieved that I'd thought to wear something decent to the store. Normally, I'd just slap on some shorts and my ragged purple flip-flops to spend the day shopping. But today, figuring that Bounce was a nice place and maybe Jenelle and I would go out for lunch somewhere in the Rice Village afterward, I'd pulled out a denim skirt and a pink sleeveless shirt. Still, I felt like a sweaty mess compared to Jenelle. Oh, well. At least it was just the two of us.

I took a deep breath and yanked the pile of frizz known as my hair off of my face. It was a super-humid day, and I had a serious case of cotton-candy head. I grabbed the front of my shirt and pulled it away from my body a bit, fanning myself with it. Bounce was air-conditioned to frosty perfection, but the crisp air hadn't managed to sink into my bones yet. "This is a great store," I said, looking around. The far wall was painted apple green, but the rest of the store was a bright, clean white. At the front was a large makeup counter, where an attractive woman with short black hair stood by in a black smock to help people try out products. Along the side walls were racks and racks of beautiful clothing, and the center was lined with painted white wooden shelves holding soft cashmere sweaters in a rainbow of colors. Everything looked fresh and inviting, and even the air had a light, sweet smell — as if the store was wearing expensive perfume.

"The formal dresses are at the back of the

store," Jenelle said, starting toward the bright green wall. "The others are already in the dressing rooms."

"Ooh, this is so pretty," I said, reaching for a pink chiffon dress with a sequined hem. But my hand stopped in midair as her words penetrated my skull. "Wait — others?"

"Okay, tell the truth," Fiona's voice commanded a moment before the dressing room door burst open and she stepped out in a short green silk dress with straps that crisscrossed over the neckline. "Isn't this a little too Britney Spears in Las Vegas?"

My heart sank. Fiona was here? Of course. Jenelle had said we would be shopping for Fiona's party. I should have known she'd come along.

Jenelle's mouth twisted to one side. "Or maybe a little Christina Aguilera on tour in Tokyo?"

Fiona looked at me. "It looks nice," I told her, but she just huffed in my direction and slammed back into the dressing room. Actually, I'd thought the dress looked fantastic. Not that anyone cared about my opinion.

"Oh, I didn't get a chance to see," Lucia's voice griped from the door next to Fiona's. Great. The whole League was here.

My fun day with Jenelle was circling the drain.

"Actually, Amy, that dress might look good on you," Jenelle suggested. "Fiona, why don't you let Amy try it on?"

"Amy can't wear green," Fiona said from inside the dressing room. "It'll make her look even paler. No bright colors."

Jenelle rolled her eyes, but she didn't protest. Instead, she pulled a pale yellow dress off the rack and hooked it over the door of the empty dressing room. "Do you like this?" she asked, pulling the pink dress I'd been eyeing off the rack. "It'll look really nice against your skin."

"Aren't you trying anything?" I asked her.

Jenelle shook her head. "I've had my dress for months — I get to go on buying trips with Mom, so I found my outfit in Paris."

"Wow," I said, only half because of Paris. The other half was because of the pale blue dress Jenelle had just pulled from the rack. It looked like a piece of origami — folded in these really cool structural shapes. It was sleeveless and knee-length. I couldn't help touching one of the folds on the bodice as Jenelle hooked it onto the dressing room door.

"How's this?" Lucia asked as she stepped out in a black goddess-style dress with only one shoulder strap. It had accordion pleats and skimmed her figure perfectly.

"Gorgeous," Jenelle announced, and I nodded.

"Really?" Lucia's dark eyes gleamed, and she gave a twirl. "I think I love it." She said it just like that — no question mark.

"Let me see," Fiona insisted, stepping out of her dressing room in a gold flapper-style dress. A frown line appeared between her eyebrows as she gave Lucia an appraising look. "It's okay," she said finally. "But the black's a little boring."

Lucia looked crushed.

"We have the same dress in maroon," Jenelle offered quickly.

"Try it," Fiona commanded, and Jenelle hurried off to find the dress as Lucia skulked back into her dressing room.

I decided to get started, so I took the three dresses and stepped into the small space. Every wall was mirrored, and there was a wide, cushioned bench to sit on. There was also a small table offering a basket of mints and several small bottles of water. Nice.

I tried on the pink dress, but I didn't even need to show it to the others to know that it was all wrong. I looked like I was auditioning for a part as a bonbon in *The Nutcracker*.

Next up was the pale yellow, but that dress made me feel like an egg. I peeled it off and stepped carefully into the blue origami dress. It looked great, but the folds were getting lost in the wild tangle of my frizzy hair. Pulling a hair clip from my bag, I twisted my hair up into a knot and fastened it at the back of my head. There. That looked a lot better.

When I stepped out of the dressing room, Jenelle actually gasped. "You look amazing!" she cried. She was standing with Lucia, who really did look amazing in the maroon version of the goddess dress. (I hate to admit it, but Fiona'd had a point about the color — the deep purple-red really brought out the warmth of Lucia's eyes.) She nodded.

"Yeah, you look really elegant?" Lucia put in. "I really like your hair like that?"

A cool tingle spread throughout my body. I felt like I was floating. . . . I don't think I'd ever felt so pretty.

"Fiona!" Jenelle called, pounding on the door to her dressing room. "Come and see Amy!"

Before I had a chance to skitter back into my dressing room, Fiona stepped out wearing an orange bubble-skirt dress with a tight bodice. The color made her black hair look extra glossy. When she saw me, she touched her chin and leaned against the door frame, a scowl stamped across her face. She held out a finger and traced a circle in the air. "Twirl," she ordered.

Feeling like a bug under a magnifying glass, I spun around slowly. *She hates it,* I thought. *I'm going to spend the day trying on dresses, and Fiona is going to hate every single one.* . . . This was not how I pictured this day.

But when I turned back to face her, Fiona did something I'd never seen her do before: She actually smiled. We're talking a genuine smile — there was nothing fake or mean about it. It actually made her look really pretty.

"That's it," she announced. "That's the outfit. You look fabulous, Amy. That dress was made for you."

"It fits you perfectly," Jenelle gushed, tugging a little at the hem to straighten it.

"You, like, have to get it?" Lucia put in.

I looked at myself in the mirror. It really *is* perfect, I thought. It hit my waist in a way that made me look like I had a figure, and the fabric had a slight shimmer that made my skin look rosy. I hadn't really planned to get a dress, but I'd brought along all of my birthday-slash-babysitting money, just in case — three hundred and twenty-six dollars. *I guess I can part with a hundred or so,* I thought.

Then I looked at the price tag.

And nearly fainted.

"It's four hundred dollars!" I gasped, looking up at Fiona.

"So?" she asked.

"It's not four hundred," Jenelle corrected, pointing at a tasteful sign placed above the rack that she'd pulled the dress from. "It's thirty percent off."

That was still two hundred eighty dollars.

"That's, like, a great deal?" Lucia exclaimed. "That's a Louise Stillton dress!"

"And it's silk," Jenelle added. "You can wear it again."

"You mean, if I get invited to the Oscars?" I joked. *Right. Where on earth am I going to wear this dress again?* I needed to save at least *some* of my money for normal clothes — stuff I could wear to school.

"You're not going to find *anything* decent for less than that," Fiona put in. Then she turned and shut the door to her dressing room. Final answer.

I looked to Jenelle for help, but she was biting her lip. "Look," she said in a low voice. "I could probably get my mom to take another ten percent off. But, seriously, that dress is perfect. And parties like this don't happen every day."

"It's going to be huge," Lucia agreed. "Don't you want to look your best?"

I sighed. They definitely had a point. The dress *was* great. If I got this dress, I'd fit right in with the rest of the League. *You have the funds,* I told myself. *Why not splurge . . . just this once?*

Over my shoulder, I could see Jenelle's face in the mirror. She looked hopeful and maybe a little worried. *She doesn't want this to turn into another huge fight with Fiona,* I realized. *And maybe she has a point.*

"Okay," I said at last. "Okay, I'll take it."

"What's going on?" I asked as I walked into the living room a few hours later. Elise was sitting on my couch, watching a DVD. It was a dumb comedy called *Don't Even!* that she and I had seen last year. It was kind of funny, but not exactly something I expected her to be watching again . . . at my house . . . without me. But when she looked up, I could see that her eyes were puffy and red, and she let out a pathetic little sniffle. Instantly,

135

all of my crankiness about shopping with the League evaporated. "Are you okay?"

"Your brother let me in," Elise said, blowing her nose into a tissue with a loud honk. "He said you'd be home soon — I hope it's okay —" She pressed the PAUSE button, and the actors froze on the screen.

"Of course it is," I said, putting my bag down beside the couch and settling into the empty space beside her. "What's up?"

Her voice quivered a little when she said, "Blake and I broke up." Then she blew her nose again.

"Oh, Elise." I put an arm around her shoulders and pulled her into a hug. "That's awful."

Elise nodded, and tears spilled over her lower lids, onto her cheeks. "It's just so out of the blue, you know? One minute, everything was going great, and the next minute, we got into an argument about cheese —"

"Cheese?" I repeated, wondering how in the world anyone could argue about cheese.

Elise rolled her eyes. "Don't even ask. I said something about the way he chews, and it got totally out of control." She took a shaky breath. "I just . . . really needed some cheering up." She looked up at me with her big, watery eyes, and warmth rushed through me. I know it's horrible, but at that moment, I was just so happy to get my friend back that I was almost a little, tiny, *teensy* bit glad that she'd broken up with Blake. I mean, of course I didn't want Elise to be sad. But it did feel good to remember that Elise and I really were good friends — and she needed me. Just like I needed her.

"I'm actually really glad you're here," I said.

"Yeah?" Elise smiled a little, although her eyes were still sad.

I blew out a sigh. As I put my feet up on the coffee table, my toe knocked a small tower of funny DVDs on the table. Elise had brought over a whole stack. Clearly, she wanted to hang out all afternoon, which was more than fine with me. "Yeah," I admitted. "I've been having kind of a hard time dealing with this girl at my school, Fiona. She's really —"

"Fiona," Elise repeated. "That's the name of the waitress who gave Blake and me our smoothies the other day." Her eyes filled with tears again.

"Oh." I didn't really know how to respond to that. *Should I go on with my story?*

"We were having so much fun." Elise's voice cracked.

Okay, forget Fiona, I thought. Elise clearly

couldn't deal with hearing about my problems at that moment, which was perfectly understandable. "Hey," I said suddenly, "what you need is some sugar therapy. Ice cream?"

"That would be perfect." Elise sounded really grateful.

"Just sit here on the couch with your movie, and I'll be back in a sec, okay?" I hauled myself off the couch and hurried toward the kitchen. "We've got peppermint fudge," I called, pulling an almost-full pint from the freezer. I knew it was Elise's favorite flavor.

"Perfect!" she yelled back.

I scooped some into two bowls and added chocolate sauce to Elise's — the way she likes it. But when I walked back into the living room, she was on her cell.

"Yeah?" she said brightly. "Me too. Oh, me too! I know. I know!" She laughed slightly and gave me a wink as I set her bowls on the table and took a bite of my ice cream. "That was so dumb. Yeah. Where are you? Really? Cool! Okay. Okay. Okay. Me too. Okay. Okay, bye." She clicked her phone closed, and before I even had a chance to ask, she said, "That was Blake! He totally apologized!"

"Really?" I said. "That's great!"

"He's at True Moo Ice Cream." Elise dabbed

138

quickly at her eyes. "He wants me to meet him so we can talk."

"Oh," I said. I glanced at her bowl of ice cream on the table, which had already started to melt.

"You don't mind, right?" Elise grabbed my hand and gave it a squeeze. "This is really, really important."

What was I going to say? Of *course* I wanted her to stay. But she looked so excited and happy. . . . "I totally understand," I said.

"You're the best," Elise said, reaching over to give me a hug. It was kind of awkward, because my bowl of ice cream was between us. "Thank you so much." Elise stood up and started for the door. Suddenly, she turned back to face me. "Do I look okay?" she asked.

Her mascara had worn off from the crying, but Elise really doesn't need to wear makeup. Her cocoa-colored skin is flawless, and her super-long lashes looked just as luscious without the mascara. I could tell she rushed out of the house this morning. Elise is usually an "outfit" girl, but today she just had on khaki shorts and a yellow tank top. But it didn't matter. "You look beautiful," I told her.

She flashed me a grateful smile. "You're such a good friend," she told me.

"That's what I always tell people."

Laughing, Elise walked out the door. "I'll call you." She gave me a quick wave before pulling it closed.

With a sigh, I turned back to the movie and pressed PLAY on the remote control. *What the heck?* I thought as I took another spoonful of ice cream. I don't have anything better to do.

"Hey — what's on?" Kirk asked as he walked into the room. "It's *Don't Even!* Turn it up, this scene is hilarious." He vaulted over the couch as I increased the volume.

On the screen, a teenage guy was running around trying to catch a runaway chicken. Kirk cracked up, then pointed to the half-melted bowl of ice cream on the table. "You eating this?"

"Go crazy," I told him. "It's been abandoned."

"Elise left? So what are you doing?"

I pointed my chin toward the screen. "Cheering myself up after spending two hundred forty dollars."

"What?" Kirk screeched. He grabbed the remote from my hand and pressed PAUSE. "What the heck did you *buy*? A car?"

I snorted. "You wish. No, I got a dress."

"A dress?" Kirk gave me his patented "Are You Nuts?" look. It features scrunched up eyebrows, lips almost touching his nose, and huge eyes. Quite a sight. "*One* dress? How did that happen?"

"I'm going to this party, and I kind of . . . got pressured into it," I admitted.

"You?" Kirk dipped his spoon into the ice cream and shoveled a huge bite into his mouth. "How fat mappen?" he asked, his lips twisting around the ice cream.

"I don't know. This new school is so weird." My bowl was empty, so I reached out for a spoonful of Kirk's, but he slapped my hand away.

"Mine," he said. He yanked the bowl away and crouched over it, protecting the ice cream with his body. Mr. Generosity, that's my brother. "What's so different?"

"It's just — it's like I don't know the rules." I shook my head. "I'm still trying to figure out how to fit in. And I guess I just feel like this party is my big chance."

Kirk thought about that for a moment. Finally, he swallowed the ice cream in his mouth and said, "Well . . . can I see the dress?"

I sighed. "Sure." Standing up, I pulled it out of the bag and held it up against my shoulders.

Kirk pursed his lips. The spoon in my bowl rattled as he put his huge feet up on the table. "It *is* cool," he admitted.

"I know." I folded it carefully and placed it back in the bag. "Two hundred forty dollars of cool."

"Could be two hundred forty dollars of ugly," Kirk pointed out.

My brother, the philosopher, I thought as we both settled back on the couch to finish the movie.

CHAPTER EIGHT

League Rule #8:
When in doubt, fake it.

"What's a ferro-fluid again?" Anderson bit his lip as he stared down at the flash cards we were making to study for our first science test.

"It's basically a liquid magnet," I told him.

He blew out a frustrated sigh and his blond bangs fluttered for a moment, then settled. "Why can't they just call it that and stop ruining my life?"

"Well, they kind of did," I told him. "Fluid means liquid, of course. And *ferrus* is the Latin word for iron, which is attracted to magnets."

Anderson gave me a blank look. "Is that supposed to be helpful?"

I laughed a little, then zipped my lips under the stern gaze of the librarian. We were sitting at a table near the back of Masterwood Library, Allington's crown jewel. It's a slick new four-story circular building with a high, vaulted ceiling. About a third of the wall on either side of the entrance is lined with floor-to-ceiling windows, and the rest is furnished with blond wood shelves, simple tables and chairs in an elegant modern design, and sleek computer terminals. My dad actually prefers to do his research here sometimes. He says that the resources are better than the ones at his university.

"I just don't understand why these facts won't stay in my brain," Anderson said as he flipped through the colorful stack of flash cards. "If you weren't my lab partner, I'd probably flunk this test. I may flunk it, anyway," he added as an afterthought.

Something about the way he said it, cracked me up. Anderson had really grown on me.

It was easy to see why Jenelle liked him so much. *Jenelle . . .*

Hmm. . . .

Maybe it's time to launch Operation Get Together.

"You won't flunk. Besides, uh . . . there are

plenty of other people you could study with," I told Anderson. "Like Jenelle. She's really good at science, too."

"Not as good as you," Anderson said, adding something to the back of his ferro-fluid flash card.

"No, she is! And —" *What else? What else? What else? Okay, be subtle,* I told myself. "And she's got really pretty hair, don't you think?"

Anderson cocked his head. "I guess it is pretty shiny."

Pretty shiny? Score! "Oh, and she can be totally funny, too," I went on. "She said the funniest thing the other day —"

"Yeah?" Anderson leaned forward across the table. "What?"

Oh, great. Now I'd completely dug myself into a hole. Of course Jenelle hadn't actually said anything funny. I was just trying to get Anderson interested in her. "Um, you had to be there," I told him quickly. "But it was truly hilarious."

"Yeah, she can be funny," Anderson said.

Super-score! This was going so great, I just couldn't stop myself. "So . . . are you, uh, going to Fiona's party?" I asked.

"Oh, definitely," Anderson said. He leaned back in his chair, twirling a pen through his fingers. "It's going to be the bash of the year."

"I heard that a lot of people are going as boy-girl couples," I said. Okay, I know this was pushing the envelope of "subtle." But if I could get Anderson to ask Jenelle to the party, I'd be such a rock star! Number one, Jenelle would have a date with the guy of her dreams, and she'd probably want to be my friend forever. And two, Fiona would have to deal with it! Mwah-hah-hah-hah-hah! I was so in love with my own evil plan that I pressed. "So, are you thinking of taking anyone?"

Anderson lifted one shoulder, then let it dip. "I don't know. . . . I hadn't really thought about it. . . ."

Should I just tell him to ask Jenelle? I thought. I was debating whether that would be breaking my promise to her when Anderson said, "Hey, why don't we go together?"

For a moment, I thought that his words had gotten garbled, or that he was speaking a foreign language or something. "What?" It was half word, half gasp.

"It would be fun," Anderson said. He put down his pencil and leaned toward me. "Don't you think? I mean, you're going anyway, right?" His blue eyes were locked on me, and I felt like a butterfly that someone had pinned to a wall.

146

Oh.

No.

A thousand thoughts crowded my brain at once: *How can I say no? How could I say yes? What the heck were you thinking? Jenelle's going to die! Way to be subtle! Why did you have to get involved? You're dead!*

"I . . ." My mouth was completely dry. This wasn't what was supposed to happen at all!

Anderson looked away, a slight blush creeping up his neck. "It's no big deal," he said quickly. "I mean, if you don't want to —"

"No, no! It would be fun!" I babbled before I even had a chance to stop myself. "Of course!" I felt my own blush turning my face into a hot tomato. *What have you done?* screamed one part of my brain. *Well, what else was I supposed to do?* another part screamed back. Then I gave this little nervous giggle that probably made me sound completely insane.

"Great!" Anderson seemed relieved. "Okay, cool. So, I'll pick you up at around seven?"

"Perfect," I told him. Which was a total lie, of course.

This situation was about as far from perfect as you can get.

Here is the noise I heard when I walked out of the library: *whiiiiiir, scraaaaape, thunkthunk*. Mitchie hopped off her skateboard and popped the rear so that it shot into her hand.

"Isn't grinding your skateboard on the library steps forbidden?" I asked her. She looked up at me with a grin, so I added, "I'd like to make a citizen's arrest."

"I wasn't grinding on the steps," Mitchie insisted. "I was grinding on the railing around the flower beds."

"Gerardo would strangle you if he saw that," I pointed out, taking a seat on the steps. They were warm from the sun.

Mitchie lifted her shoulders in a quick shrug. "Only if I fall in the flowers. I just try to fall toward the concrete." She tucked her board under her arm and climbed toward me, brushing off the step before she sat down. In her cool turquoise hooded knit shirt and black leggings, she was the cleanest, girliest skater chick I'd ever seen. "So — how's it going?"

I rolled my eyes.

"What? Depressed because our detention adventure is over?" Mitchie joked.

"No, it's just . . ." I hesitated.

148

Mitchie cocked her head. "What?"

"It's just that this boy asked me to this party, and he's really nice and all, but I kind of don't want to go with him. And I have to wear this expensive dress, which is a total waste of money, and I'm starting to think that this party is going to be a total drag. . . ." A shudder ran through my body. "I have no idea why I'm even going."

"Hmm." Mitchie balanced her skateboard across her knees and leaned back on her elbows. "Is this party . . . by any chance . . . being thrown by Fiona Von Steig?"

I leaned forward to plant my chin on my fists. "That's the one."

"Ah." Mitchie nodded, biting her bottom lip thoughtfully. "And was the dress . . . by any chance . . . one that Fiona picked out for you?"

"Kind of," I admitted. "How did you know that?"

A long moment passed. "I actually know Fiona pretty well," Mitchie said at last. "We used to be really good friends."

"Really?" I asked. I tried to picture it, but it seemed pretty hard to believe. I'd never even seen them glance in each other's direction.

"I can't do anything about your boy situation, but I may have a solution to your dress problem. Do you have a pen?"

"Sure." I dug a ballpoint and a small notebook out of my backpack and handed them over.

"This place isn't far from here," she said as she scribbled down an address. "Tell them that I sent you." She handed me the notebook.

"Divine?" I asked, reading the name on the page.

"It truly is," Mitchie promised.

I eyed the address. "It's only a few blocks from my house."

"Then you have no excuse not to check it out."

A horn honked. It was my dad, behind the wheel of our minivan. "I've got to go," I said.

"Good luck," Mitchie told me, nodding at the notebook in my hand.

I tucked it carefully into my bag. "Thanks. Hey, are you going to Fiona's party?"

"Wouldn't miss it."

"Cool." I yanked open the passenger side door and climbed in.

Mitchie picked up her board as we drove away and headed down the steps. To attack the flower rail again, no doubt.

"So, how was your day?" Dad asked as he pulled into the steady stream of traffic.

"Pretty good," I told him. I eased the notebook out of the outer pocket of my bag and rechecked

150

the address Mitchie had given me. "Hey, Dad?" I asked. "Do you mind dropping me off a few blocks from home?"

A silver bell tinkled cheerfully as I walked through Divine's front door. To the left were café tables and a small counter for coffee and cookies. To the right were racks and racks of clothes. A spiral staircase led to the second level, where even more clothes, hats, and bags were neatly hung, waiting for inspection. *Why did Mitchie send me here?* I wondered. It was a nice place, sure, but the clothes looked kind of expensive.

A woman in a black-and-white Chanel suit was standing in front of the clothes counter, tapping her long nails on the glass. "How're we doing, sweetheart?" she drawled.

"Is that everything, Mrs. Pelling?" asked the girl behind the counter, flashing a bright smile. She had waist-length hair in a gorgeous shade of brownish-red, and looked about my age. There was something familiar about her, but I couldn't quite place where I'd seen her before.

"Everything until next season." Mrs. Pelling tugged at the large diamond at her earlobe. Her hair was done in the blond helmet-style that the older ladies at our church seem to love . . . but Mrs. Pelling didn't have any wrinkles.

"Okay." The girl finished filling out a receipt and handed it over to Mrs. Pelling. "We'll give you a call once everything has sold."

"Thanks, darlin'." Mrs. Pelling gave the girl a wink, then strolled toward the door.

"Wait!" I called to her. "You forgot your clothes!"

Mrs. Pelling gave me a funny look. Then she burst into laughter. "Hoo! That's a good one! Take care, now!" She yanked open the door and strode out.

I turned toward the auburn-haired girl behind the counter, who was busy placing an elegant embroidered jacket on a hanger. "Is she picking them up later or something?"

The girl cocked her head, like she couldn't quite make out what I was saying. "We're a consignment shop," she said. "At the end of each season, all the socialites in Houston drop off their clothes. When they sell, we give them half the money." Her brown eyes twinkled. "Not that they need it."

"Oh." I looked around the store, feeling kind of silly. "This is the nicest thrift store I've ever seen," I said, eyeing the marble floors.

The girl laughed. "We prefer the term 'resale,'" she said. "So, can I help you find anything?"

"Well . . . I'm looking for a dress. . . ."

"Casual or formal?"

"Formal," I said. "But not froufrou."

"We've got some great ones over here." The girl stepped out from behind the counter and led me toward the rear of the store. She was wearing a stylish dress in a geometric print. "I'm Kiwi, by the way."

"Kiwi?" I repeated.

"Actually, it's Cairdwyn," Kiwi explained. "But my little brother couldn't pronounce it, so it got a little mangled."

"I'm Amy," I told her.

"Great to meet you," Kiwi said, pulling a violet dress off the rack. "What do you think of this?"

I frowned slightly, thinking about Fiona's no-bright-color mandate. "I think maybe something a little less . . . intense. Color-wise."

"Okay." Kiwi put the dress back, flipped through a few hangers, and pulled out a mint-green column dress. "This?"

"Pretty." I took it from her, admiring the delicate beadwork at the neck. "This still has the original price tag."

"A lot of them do," Kiwi said, yanking two other dresses from the rack. "The women who come here shop like mad. They've got more clothes than places to wear them. What do you think of these two?" In her right hand was a lovely, fitted beige taffeta dress, and in her left was a blue dress with origami folds.

I gasped. "I just bought this at Bounce! The exact same dress!"

"Really?" Kiwi looked impressed. "You must have paid some serious money for it."

"Tell me about it," I said, pulling the dress from her hand. "It's the same size!" I flipped over the price tag. "Omigosh — sixty dollars?" My head swam. I could buy this dress and return the other one to Bounce. I didn't even need to try it on. The exact same dress — for a fourth of the price! *Mitchie, you are my hero,* I thought.

"Lucky you," Kiwi said. "I wish we had it in my size." She folded her arms across her chest. "You look really familiar to me. . . . Aren't you in my Spanish class?"

"That's where I've seen you before!" I cried. I couldn't believe I hadn't placed her. I'd noticed Kiwi from the first day of school — she wore a different cool outfit every day. *I'll bet she gets her clothes right here,* I realized. "You sit near the back."

"Well . . . Senora Duggan has kind of a . . ." she leaned toward me and whispered, ". . . *volume-control* problem."

"I know," I agreed. "I always feel like she's shouting directly into my skull. So, how did you get this job?"

"Oh, I've worked here since birth, practically. My parents own the place." She placed the other dresses back on the rack and said, "Do you need anything else? Some accessories? We just got in a bunch of cool shoes — some Christian Louboutins that are still in the box. And some really great jewelry." Quickly, she walked over to the glass case and pointed at a necklace of pale blue and green crystals.

"Perfect!"

"Do you want to take a look at bags?" Kiwi asked. "Someone just brought in a Prada that would look amazing with that dress."

I couldn't believe it. Just five minutes ago, I was broke, singing the Expensive Dress Blues. And now — I had a dress *and* some decent money to spend. *I'll bet I can get everything for less than half of what it cost me just to get the dress at Bounce,* I thought. *So why not get a nice bag? And maybe I should get some school clothes, too.* "Kiwi, show me everything you've got."

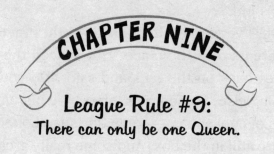

CHAPTER NINE

League Rule #9:
There can only be one Queen.

Jenelle, I just want you to know that Anderson and I are only going to the party together as friends, I rehearsed mentally as the manicurist filed my nails. Her name tag read ANNE. *He's not interested in me at all, and by the way he said that you have really shiny hair. . . .*

I snuck a peek at Jenelle, who was sitting nearby. Her blond hair hung in a curtain, hiding her face, so I couldn't read her expression. But I was nervous. She'd barely said a word to me since we arrived at the spa. I really wanted to talk to her about Anderson, but she was sitting between

Lucia and Fiona, so I decided to wait until I could get her alone.

The manicurist, Anne, broke into my thoughts. "Y'all going to a party?" Anne painted a clear base coat onto my index fingernail in precise strokes.

"Yeah, it's Fiona's birthday." I nodded in Fiona's direction, but she didn't glance up. She was too busy flipping through a copy of *Vogue* with one hand while the manicurist worked on the other. "Actually, this spa trip is a present from Lucia," I went on. "She paid for all of us."

"How sweet," Anne said.

"I know." Honestly, I'd nearly fainted when I got the e-mail from Lucia inviting me to La Luxe for a manicure along with the rest of the League. The spa was the most expensive in Houston. Normally, I wouldn't have even been able to afford to set foot in there. For a while, I'd been worried that maybe it was another practical joke, but when I arrived, the woman behind the counter explained that Lucia's parents had paid for everything in advance — including tips — so I should just relax and enjoy my day. Then she gave me a glass of "mango-infused lemonade" and had me take a "journey of the senses" to choose the kind of hand lotion I wanted. The whole place was decorated in blue and gold, and there were enormous crystal chandeliers everywhere. It was gorgeous, and I was starting to understand what was fun about being in the League.

As they say, membership has its privileges.

"Color?" Anne asked.

"Oh, um . . ."

"Over there." She pointed to a rack just beyond her shoulder.

I stood up and walked over to face the hundreds of colors — more shades of red, plum, beige, pink, and taupe than I'd ever imagined. *What's the difference between Sahara Drama and Oasis Sand?* I wondered as I glanced at the labels. They looked exactly the same to me.

That's when I noticed the other rack — a smaller one set lower and to the right. This was where all of the fun colors were — a bright grasshopper green, sunflower yellow, midnight black with sparkles, cornflower blue. . . .

Hmm, cornflower blue . . .

"I need to talk to you," Jenelle whispered, appearing behind me. She didn't look at me as she said it. She just kept her eyes glued to the rack of pinks in front of her.

"I need to talk to you, too," I said, my heart pounding a fierce beat. "Listen, I —"

Jenelle's eyes snapped onto mine. "My mom told me that you returned the dress last night," she said. "Is that true?"

"W-w-what?" I stammered.

"The blue dress you bought for Fiona's party. Mom said that it came back."

"I — I — yes, but —"

"Amy, why do you keep making things hard for yourself?" Jenelle snapped. She wrapped her fingers around my arm. I felt like I was caught in a vise.

"Don't worry, I —"

"I *am* worried, okay?" Jenelle said. "Things were just starting to click. Fiona was getting used to you, Lucia invited you along today, and now . . ."

A sudden flash of anger shot through me like a burning arrow. "Why does it matter what dress I wear, anyway? Isn't it my choice?"

Jenelle's eyes narrowed. "This isn't just about you, Amy, don't you get it? If you show up at the party in a dress that Fiona doesn't like, you'll be making *my* life hard."

"Jenelle," I said gently, "is the dress really such a huge deal?"

When she turned to look at me, I saw that tears were pooling at the rims of her eyes. "I heard about Anderson," she hissed. "I thought you said you didn't like him!"

"What's going on here?" Fiona asked as she walked up to the rack. "Having trouble deciding which color?"

Jenelle released my arm and blinked quickly, clearing the tears in her eyes. "Uh . . . yes," she said awkwardly. "Amy was just helping me choose between Ballerina Blush and Stardust." She pointed to two identical shades of pink.

"Oh, Stardust has *way* too much pink in it," Fiona said. "Definitely go with Ballerina Blush."

"That's what I was thinking," Jenelle said, pulling the shade from the rack.

"I think I'll go with that, too." Fiona smiled. "Listen, Amy, there was a favor I wanted to ask you."

"What did I miss?" Lucia asked. Her eye fell on the small bottle in Jenelle's hand. "Is that Ballerina Blush?"

"We're all getting it," Fiona announced.

"What's the favor?" I asked impatiently. I really wished that Fiona and Lucia would leave, so that I could talk to Jenelle and explain the Anderson situation.

"I need some help with a magic trick." Fiona toyed with a deep burgundy shade, her glossy lips

160

puckered in a slight frown. "When everyone walks into the party, they'll be facing a stage. I've hired a magician to do a trick where I appear in a glass box. There's only one problem. . . ."

"The magician is, like, hairy?" Lucia volunteered. "And completely sweaty and gross? And has, like, a mustache?"

"I was wondering if you could be the magician," Fiona finished. "It's easy — all you have to do is cover the large glass box with a velvet cloth. Then I'll come up from a trapdoor in the floor, and you can take off the cloth and let me out."

"It'll be like she appeared from nowhere?" Lucia said. "It's going to be so cool!"

"Normally, I wouldn't even ask you," Fiona admitted, setting the burgundy color back into place. "But Lucia and Jenelle are going to be busy checking the guest list —"

"It's no problem," I said quickly. "It sounds like fun." Actually, it really did. Besides, I wanted to show Jenelle that I wasn't trying to be difficult. . . .

"Great," Fiona said. "Get there a little early, and I'll show you what to do. It's not a big deal. I'm sure that even you can handle it." She tossed her long hair over one shoulder and stalked off.

Jenelle cast a quick warning glance over her shoulder as she and Lucia followed Fiona back to their seats. I sighed. Okay, so that hadn't gone at all as I'd planned. I hadn't had a chance to say word one about Anderson. . . .

"That's *such* a fun color," Anne said as I took my seat across from her.

I looked down at the bottle in my hand. I'd completely forgotten that I was still holding the cornflower blue polish. I hesitated a moment. Everyone else was getting Ballerina Blush. . . .

Oh, forget it, I decided. I liked the blue. "It goes with my dress," I explained, passing it to her. Now I had two things to explain to Jenelle: Anderson and the dress. Hanging out with the League was becoming seriously complicated.

Membership may have its privileges, I thought, *but it sure has its problems, too.*

"What do you think?" I asked Pizza as I swabbed clear lip gloss over my pink lipstick. "Too much shine?"

Pizza cocked her head, and the tips of her white ears flopped in a very "Do I Look Like I Know Anything About Fashion?" expression. I stroked the back of her fuzzy neck, and she leaned happily against my calf. "I don't know why I ever wanted to go to this party," I whispered. I'd been trying to call Jenelle all day, but she hadn't picked up.

Indifferent to my problems, Pizza ambled stiffly toward the little bed I keep in the corner for her. She flopped across it and fell asleep almost instantly.

Just then, my door flung open. "There's an eighteen-wheeler out front to pick you up," Kirk said. "Hey . . ." He cocked his head in a way that looked surprisingly like Pizza had a moment before. "You look . . . kind of good."

This, from my brother, was a high compliment. "Really?" I said. "Do you think that the hair is okay?" I'd styled it into a low bun, but had let a few tendrils stay loose around my face. I wasn't sure if it looked romantic, or sort of like half of my hair had escaped the frizz farm.

"I already gave you one compliment," Kirk said. "Don't push it." He shuffled down the hall.

I grabbed my green purse (a medium-sized duffel-style . . . not as huge as I usually carry, but roomy enough for all of my essential items) and headed for the living room. Anderson was standing beside the coffee table, chatting with my mom. They stopped talking when I walked in, and Anderson beamed.

"Oh, Amy, you look beautiful!" Mom gushed.

"Great dress," Anderson agreed. He was looking pretty great, too, in his tuxedo with a green cumberbund and matching bow tie. "This is for you." He held out a plastic box. Inside was a vibrant purple orchid.

"Thanks," I said, not sure what to do with it. I looked to my mom for help.

"It's a corsage," she explained. "You can wear it on your dress or on your wrist."

"It's so pretty." I pulled out the flower, which was attached to a piece of elastic. "Hey, do you think I could wear it on my ankle?"

Anderson grinned. "That would be *awesome*."

I took off my shoe and pulled the flower over my foot. It looked cool there — a pretty anklet.

"Ready?" Anderson asked.

"Oh, let me get a picture," Mom said. She snapped a couple of photos, and then we walked outside.

"Whoa." I actually gasped when I saw what was waiting for us. It was a white stretch *Hummer*. Kirk had been right — it really did look like there was a big rig parked in our driveway.

"Pretty cool, right?" Anderson said proudly as the chauffeur opened the door for us.

"This backseat is as big as my room," I replied.

Anderson laughed, but I really wasn't kidding. It was huge. There was even a high-def TV.

"Do you want a Coke or something?" Anderson pulled open a wooden door that turned out to be a fridge.

"I'm afraid I'll spill it on myself." I settled into the plush leather seat. "If we go over a bump."

"Good thinking." Anderson had taken a Dr. Pepper, but he put it back.

We sat there for a minute, neither one of us knowing what to say. Silence settled over the car. I could hear the tires humming beneath us.

"What's that?" I asked, pointing to a remote control.

"Oh, it's for the TV," he said. "And for this." He aimed it at the roof, and a panel pulled back.

"A sunroof!" I stood on the seat, popping my head through the car's ceiling.

Anderson did the same. "I feel like a dog," he said as the breeze whipped past our faces. People on the streets stared at us as the Hummer rolled past them, two heads floating through its roof.

We flopped back onto the seat, laughing.

"I've never done that before," Anderson said.

"I've never even been in a limo before," I told him.

"Really?" Anderson looked shocked. Which was kind of funny, considering that he'd just been to my house. I mean, it was pretty obvious that we weren't exactly rich. "Not even with Jenelle or anything?" he asked.

Right. I'd forgotten that she and Fiona got a ride to school every morning in Lucia's family limo. "Well . . . we haven't really known each other that long."

Anderson shifted in his seat. "Do you — do you know if she's going with anyone to this party?" he asked.

"I don't think so," I said. My heart was pounding in my ears. "Why?"

"Oh, it's just . . ." He blushed a little.

"Do you have a crush on Jenelle?" Excitement made my voice shrieky. I sounded like a parrot.

"No," Anderson said quickly. He made a *phissh* sound and reached for the door to the fridge. But then he seemed to remember that he'd decided against drinking a soda, and shut the door again. He looked at me sheepishly. "Maybe a little," he said after a moment.

"Well, why didn't you ask her to go with you to the party?" I demanded.

Anderson thought for a minute, and it was like the idea just crept over his face — as if it had only just that moment snuck up on him. "I thought the party was just a friend thing."

"Anderson!" I punched him playfully on the shoulder.

"Do you think..." Anderson turned an even deeper shade of red. "Do you think you could find out if she likes anyone?"

Of course, my vow of silence is the only thing that kept me from shouting, *She likes* you, *you nitwit!* But I was good. "I'll talk to her at the party," I promised.

Boy, would I!

"This is amazing," I whispered as Anderson and I walked up the red carpet. The awning overhead was strung with paper lanterns, and a line of people had already formed at the entrance. It was funny — I almost didn't recognize my classmates. Everyone was dressed up and looking seriously stunning.

"Can you just, like, chill a minute?" Lucia demanded irritably as a guy in a white tuxedo hovered over her shoulder while she checked her clipboard. "Okay, you can go in." She let the guy past the velvet rope.

"Here's your VIP badge," Jenelle said, handing it over to a girl in a short pink-sequined dress.

"You can use it to get to the front row for the Eloquence show later." Jenelle looked really lovely in her white strapless dress. The bodice was tight and beaded, and the bottom flowed toward her knees in diagonals, like flower petals.

Completely forgetting that she was mad at me, I waved and shouted, "Jenelle!"

She looked up at me. Then her eyes flicked to Anderson, and she frowned down at her clipboard.

I gulped. "Listen, Fiona wanted me to tell Jenelle something about the VIP badges," I said to Anderson. "I'll be right back."

"Okay, you're all set," Jenelle was saying to a tall guy as I walked up.

"Jenelle," I whispered the minute he was out of earshot. "I have to talk to you."

"Can't you see that I'm busy?" she snapped.

"It'll just take a second." Grabbing her by the elbow, I dragged her away from her station.

"Let go," she said, twisting out of my grip.

"Fine, but you have to listen to me. Look, Anderson and I are just friends. He even told me on the way over here that he has a crush on someone else."

Jenelle's granite expression softened a little. "Who?" she whispered.

168

"You, of course," I told her. "I've been saying that all along!"

"Really?" Her voice was a squeak. "Amy, if you're lying to me . . ."

"I'm not lying!" I cried. "I wouldn't do that to you, okay? I'm not like that."

Jenelle stood there for a moment. Then, suddenly, she grabbed me, pulling me into a fierce hug. "Thank you," she whispered. "I'm really sorry I got so mad, I just —"

"Forget it. So, what are you going to do about it?" I asked her.

"I don't know." Jenelle snuck a glance in Anderson's direction, then looked back at me quickly. "Fiona might not —"

"Oh, *Fiona*." I rolled my eyes.

"Excuse me?" An eighth grade girl in a black satin sheath dress snapped her fingers in our direction. "I've been *waiting*?"

Jenelle nodded. "We'll talk later," she whispered. "And you look great, by the way." Then she hurried back to her place. I bit my lip, then slowly trudged after her. I couldn't believe that Jenelle actually cared that much about what Fiona thought.

Just before I reached the line, I felt a tap on my shoulder.

"Amy?" Scott stood there in a gray suit, look-ing . . . gorgeous.

My insides turned to goo as he smiled at me. "You look beautiful," he said. "I love your ankle corsage."

"Thanks," I breathed. "You too." Then I real-ized what I'd said. "Um, not that you're wearing an ankle corsage," I added quickly.

His lips curved into a wide smile, and for a second, it was like the rest of the world disappeared. . . .

At that moment, the line shifted, and Anderson stepped up beside me. "Hey, you're back!" he said. Then he turned to Scott. "Hi, I'm Anderson!" He held out his hand.

Scott blinked in surprise, his gaze moving from me to Anderson and back again. "Oh, hi." Scott shook his hand, but he wasn't smiling anymore. "I, uh — well, I just got here — guess I've got to get in line, like everyone else. It was good seeing you, Amy."

And then he disappeared into the crowd of beautiful people.

"That guy was really *smiling* at you," Anderson said brightly. He gave me a broad wink.

I sighed. "Yeah, but now he thinks I'm going out with someone else."

Anderson looked blank. "Who?"

I just shook my head. Not the swiftest car around the track . . . but he meant well.

"Hello?" I called, poking my head between the white velvet curtains. It hadn't been easy to make my way through the swirling party. I had to admit that the Winter Wonderland theme looked great, though. Tables were set up around the dance floor, and silver Mylar balloons were tied to the chairs. At the center of each table was an enormous, fragrant centerpiece of white lilies and roses. Sparkly white snowflakes were hung from the ceiling, and every ten minutes, fake snow floated down over the crowd. The caterers walked around in white outfits, holding white food on silver trays. I'd wanted to look at everything, but I'd told Fiona I'd help her out, so here I was. "Anybody back here?"

"There you are," Fiona snapped. "Come on, get back here quickly. I don't want anyone to see me," she added, ducking away from the curtains as I slipped through.

"You look really pretty," I told her. "I love your earrings."

Fiona was wearing a short white dress with a sapphire sash, and at her throat was the usual diamond-and-sapphire pendant, which matched her earrings perfectly. Fiona put a hand to her ear. "Birthday present," she explained. "Of course, I *asked for* a ski trip with my friends." She rolled her eyes. "But whatever. Okay, let me show you the trick."

We crossed the empty stage, and Fiona led me backstage into the wings. It was creepy and dark back there, and I couldn't help feeling like we had just walked onto the set of a horror movie. "Is this the part where you drop a sandbag on my head?" I joked.

"Only if you mess up my magic trick," Fiona replied. I wasn't sure she was kidding. "So this is the cloth," she explained, pulling a large piece of velvet from a nearby table. "You can just handle it like this and drape it over the box, like this." The box was tall, like a telephone booth, but narrower. Gracefully, Fiona flipped the velvet across the top of a clear plastic box so that it hung down evenly on all four sides. "I'll climb in through a trapdoor in the bottom, and when I'm ready, I'll knock gently on the glass from inside." Yanking the cloth aside, she stepped into the box and tapped on one of the walls to demonstrate. "Then you remove the cloth and lift the lid and *voilà.*"

"Easy peasy, mac-n-cheesy," I told her, and she glared at me. I cleared my throat. "Um, I mean, no problem."

"Okay, great. Do you mind moving the box onto the stage? I've got to make sure that my other dresses are all set."

"*Other* dresses?" I asked.

"I couldn't decide which dress to buy." Fiona tossed her hair behind her shoulders. "So I got four. I'm going to change after the trick, after the DJ, and right before the cake."

"Wow."

"I know." She smiled smugly. "They're all white with sapphire-blue trim, but they're all completely different — two of them are custom-made. I think it makes a real statement."

"It sure does," I agreed. *Yeah, the statement is, "I've got more money than brains."*

"Okay!" Fiona said brightly. "I'll see you later!"

I eyed the clear box as she flounced off to check her dresses. "How the heck am I going to move this thing by myself?" I muttered. But the answer was simple — I couldn't. I'd have to get Anderson to help me.

I had to fight my way through the curtains, and when I stepped back into the party, the volume had doubled. The place was packed! *How will I ever find Anderson?* I wondered, standing on tiptoe to peek through the crowd.

"Hey, Amy!" For a minute, I didn't even recognize Mitchie. Her hair was fluffy in the back, and she had a ladder of diamond barrettes sideways across her bangs. She looked beautiful in a structured silver dress. It was a pretty far cry from her usual skater-chick style.

"You look amazing!" I gushed.

"Eh, I can work the girlie thing once in a while," Mitchie said with a shrug.

"Have you seen Anderson Sempe anywhere? I need his help with something."

"Haven't seen him," Mitchie said, turning to help me scan the crowd. "Then again, I've only been here about five minutes. What do you need him for?"

I gestured toward the curtain behind me. "I have to move this big box onto the stage."

"I could help you with that," Mitchie said.

"Really? Oh, thanks!"

She smiled. "What are friends for?"

We hustled backstage and kicked off our heels so that we wouldn't fall over while trying to heave the box around. I mean, I personally could barely manage to walk in those things as it was. Then we set our bags down by our shoes and tackled the box.

"It's . . . heavier . . . than . . . it . . . looks," Mitchie grunted as we half-carried, half-shoved the thing toward the center of the stage.

"Just . . . a . . . little . . . farther," I gasped.

We hauled it into place and stood there, breathing heavily. "What's this for, anyway?" Mitchie asked, eyeing the box as she slipped back into her shoes.

"Magic trick," I explained. "Fiona's going to surprise everyone by appearing inside it."

"It would be better if you could make her *disappear*," Mitchie muttered.

As if drawn by the sound of her own name, Fiona chose that moment to show up. "Good, you moved it — we're going on in about five minutes. Oh, hello, Michiko. I see you've finally figured out what a dress is," she sneered, flashing her perfectly whitened teeth.

I felt Mitchie's body go rigid beside mine. "Hi, Fiona," she said. "Nice party. It's great to see the people around you having a good time, for once."

The smile dropped from Fiona's face, and her blue eyes narrowed to dangerous slits. "Your hair looks really great. I just love what you've done with those diamonds." Reaching out, she touched one of the barrettes with a fingertip, and Mitchie flinched away. "Aren't you glad I fixed that waist-length disaster for you?" Then she turned and stalked away.

For a long, long moment, neither one of us spoke. We stood there in the semidarkness, listening to the bubbling conversation beyond the curtain, the clink of silverware on china, laughter. But all of that seemed completely unreal. My head was swimming, as thoughts flew through it, fluttering like a flock of startled birds. "It was *your* hair," I said at last. "You were the girl in the story you told me — the one who was friends with Fiona. She cut off your hair."

Mitchie didn't speak, but I could see tears gathering in her eyes. Her jaw was working furiously as she struggled to keep them from escaping.

"She's so . . . *mean,*" I whispered.

Mitchie barked a laugh. "I know."

"But nobody ever calls her on it," I went on.

Mitchie gave me a sideways look. "It doesn't pay to mess with Fiona," she said. "Trust me."

She stepped through the curtains, leaving me there, alone on the stage. Inside, I could feel my blood simmering, as if someone had lit a fire beneath me and brought me to a boil. *This isn't right,* I thought. *She can't just get away with that kind of stuff!*

I knew one thing for sure. I wasn't going to let her. Not anymore.

"Are you ready for a good time?" The crowd roared. The emcee — DJ Slice — had stopped spinning tunes, and was warming up the crowd from his place behind the turntables. "All right, all right!" he cried, his gold teeth shining. "I bet y'all are wondering where the girl of the hour is!"

Another cheer went up, threatening to shake the paint off the walls. *Maybe this isn't such a good idea,* I thought, gulping hard. But it was too late.

"Well, without further ado, here's the magic that's going to make her appear!" DJ Slice called. "Put your hands together for our guest magician, Amy Flowers!"

The curtains parted and I walked out onto the stage holding the velvet cloth. A wave of cheers washed over me and a spotlight shined in my eyes, half blinding me. I could hardly see anything but a dark, rippling mass of bodies — everyone in the seventh and eighth grades at Allington. *This plan is either going to work . . .* I thought as I took a short, stiff bow . . . *or it's going to be a complete disaster. . . .*

"As you can see, this is a simple, ordinary glass box," I announced. The crowd quieted down as I shook out the velvet cloth. "I will now use my amazing powers to produce the hostess of this fabulous party!"

Whoops went up as I flapped the cloth twice, then swung it up over the glass box. It landed there with a light flutter, dropping neatly into place. "Hocus pocus!" I cried, waving my arms like a maniac. "Alacazam!"

Tap, tap.

There was my signal. "Abracadabra!" I cried, ripping off the cloth.

The crowd oohed at the sight of Fiona standing there, then burst into applause. Someone let out a deafening whistle.

Fiona glanced at me, smiling hugely. She gestured toward the door, and I moved to open it. I gave it a quick yank. Then another. I pulled harder, then tried to push. No use. The door didn't budge. "It's stuck," I said.

"What?" Fiona's voice was muffled behind the thick plastic. She shoved at the door, but it didn't open. A murmur of confusion rippled through the

178

crowd as she pounded against the clear wall with her fists then let out a furious scream.

"Hey!" someone shouted. "Someone finally put Fiona in a cage!"

The crowd cracked up.

A blue vein stood out on her forehead — her face was turning red with rage. *Gee — I hope she has enough oxygen in there,* I thought.

She pointed at me. "Get me out of here," she yelled. "Or I'll *strangle* you!" Her voice was loud enough for everyone to hear — even through the plastic.

"Maybe you'd better leave her in there!" a guy's voice cried. Fiona gaped at him. "Get out of my party!" she shrieked. A few people cracked up, and Fiona went wild-eyed. "Anyone who laughs has to leave *now*!" She pounded on the glass for added emphasis.

The crowd let out an "oooooh," and in a moment, some people at the back started to chant: "Leave her! Leave her! Leave her!"

The glare that Fiona shot in my direction was almost enough to melt a hole in the plastic between us. Almost. I gave her a little smile. *Don't worry,* I mouthed.

She looked like her head was about to blow up,

and she slammed her fist into the thick plastic again.

"Oooh, you'll hurt yourself," I said brightly. "Careful!" Then I turned to the crowd. "Well — I guess Fiona isn't quite ready to join us. I will now make her disappear again!"

The crowd started to cheer. They didn't even seem to realize that Fiona was actually stuck. They thought it was all part of the act.

I just wish I could make this disappearing act permanent, I thought as I gave Fiona a little "toodles" wave with my fingers, then flipped the velvet cloth over the box again. She didn't have any choice. Her only way out was through the trapdoor below.

I waited until I heard the trapdoor slide shut, then yanked the cloth off again. When they saw the empty box, the crowd went nuts.

"A-my!" someone shouted. "A-my! A-my!" Soon, everyone was chanting. "A-my! A-my! A-my!" I took a deep bow, and the crowd cheered so hard that I could feel the noise vibrate through my chest.

I couldn't stop smiling as the curtains closed, and DJ Slice started up the music.

That . . . I thought . . . *was* perfect.

I took a moment to drink in my triumph before heading backstage. Fiona was waiting in the wings, her arms folded across her chest, her normally beautiful face twisted into an ugly, distorted snarl. "You are *so* dead, do you hear me?" she growled. "Your life at Allington is officially *over*."

I just tossed the velvet cloth at her. "What life?" I asked.

The look of shock on her face was priceless. Her lips opened and closed, like a puppet's jaw. But she couldn't speak.

I'll bet that's the first time she's ever been speechless, I thought as I walked away. I felt a little smile creep across my lips. *I wonder how long it'll last.*

"Amy, that was awesome! Great sketch — you and Fiona cracked me up."

"Amazing — you were so hilarious! Amy, right?"

"You're classic, dude. You're the one who tossed the soda on Albermarle!"

Before the prank, I'd been afraid that people would boo me or yell at me when I left the stage. Instead, my classmates were pounding me on the back, talking to me, and laughing about the Fiona debacle — I mean, magic act — as I tried to shove my way across the dance floor.

"Hey, Amy!" A girl grabbed my hand. She was wearing an emerald-green dress and had matching streaks in her blond hair, and she was vaguely familiar. . . . "Voe Silk?" she said, pointing to herself. "Remember? You told me where to get the green dye for my hair?"

"Oh, hi!" I said. Right — the eighth-grade queen of cool.

"I just wanted to say thanks," Voe said, wrapping her arm around my shoulder as if we were best friends. "And to tell you that I thought your skit with Fiona was hysterical! The whole comedy routine — you know, she can't get out of the box, you're the bumbling magician. . . . Everyone loved it!"

"Riiiight," I said slowly. "It was all Fiona's idea."

"Obviously! It was *totally* her sense of humor. Anyway, great job! Have you ever thought about auditioning for the school musical?"

"Well, I —"

"Think about it," Voe commanded, poking me directly under the collarbone.

Before I had a chance to say that I would, a drop-dead handsome guy walked up to Voe and slung a casual arm around her waist. "Amy Flowers, you are a genius," he told me. Then they walked off toward the dance floor.

"Uh, thanks!" I called to his back, but my words were swallowed up by the music that was blasting from the speakers at every corner of the room.

Someone tapped me on the shoulder.

"Wow," Mitchie said when I turned around. I could tell by her smile that she knew Fiona getting stuck in the box wasn't part of the act. "Wow. That was brilliant."

"*Totally* brilliant," Kiwi, who was standing beside her, agreed. They were both giving me huge grins. I guess I shouldn't have been so surprised to realize that they were friends.

"Well, I heard that Fiona just loves pranks," I said, which cracked them both up.

"How did you do it?" Mitchie asked.

I pulled a small green-and-white tube from my purse. "Say hello to my little friend."

Kiwi cocked an eyebrow at me. "Why do you have Krazy Glue in your purse?"

"Oh, in case I break a heel or a fingernail, or in case one of the straps on my bag breaks. . . . Honestly, it has about a thousand uses."

"More like a thousand and one," Mitchie corrected. She gave a little snort, which sounded like an escaped laugh. But when she recovered, her expression turned serious. "You know that prank was completely demented, though, right? Fiona's going to toss you on the grill."

"Oh, well," I replied. "I guess I don't get to sit with the League at lunch on Monday."

"You can sit with us," Kiwi suggested.

"And you can eat whatever you want," Mitchie volunteered. "Even liverwurst."

I smiled at them, and they smiled back. "Sounds great," I said.

I was fifteen feet from the door when I realized that I had no way to get home. Anderson was supposed to take me, but he'd disappeared. And I absolutely didn't want to stay. *Great,* I thought. *Let's celebrate another no-cell-phone moment.*

Who can I ask?

Through the crowd on the packed dance floor, I spotted Jenelle. She was slow-dancing with Anderson, her eyes closed and a dreamy expression on her face. *Wow, she really is taller than he is,* I thought as I watched them. Anderson only came up to her neck. As they swayed in a circle, Anderson caught my eye over her shoulder and gave me a thumbs-up. I thumbs-upped him back. They were really cute together.

Okay, I'm not about to ask them, I thought. A happy little tingle ran through my body at the thought of the good deed I'd done. *At least Jenelle is happy.* And I still thought that we could be friends — someday. That is, I hoped so.

"Are you okay?" asked a soft voice beside me.

It was Scott. He leaned toward me slightly and peered into my face. "You seem . . . thoughtful."

A familiar giddy shiver ran through me at the sight of him. "I guess I am," I admitted.

"Is it . . ." Scott jutted his chin toward the dance floor. "Is it because your date is dancing with someone else?" His deep brown eyes were full of sympathy.

"My *date*?" I repeated. "You mean *Anderson*? Please." I rolled my eyes. "He's barely my lab partner."

"Oh." Suddenly, his eyes brightened. "Oh!"

We stood there for a moment, just smiling at each other. I felt like . . . well, I felt like I'd never be able to stop, like that grin had taken over my body. And all I can say about Scott is . . . he looked the way I felt. "So . . ." he said after a moment. "Um . . . do you want to dance?"

I knew that I should say no. *I should leave,* I thought. *Fiona doesn't want me here. . . .*

Then again, am I seriously going to pass up the opportunity to dance with Scott at the biggest bash of the year?

Um, no *way.*

"Scott," I said, "I'd love to."

His hand was warm as he grabbed mine and led me out onto the dance floor. The music had changed and now the beat was pounding — DJ Slice was playing some cool hip-hop, and everyone on the floor was moving. *This is amazing!* I thought as fake snow fluttered down from the ceiling. *It's truly magical.* But suddenly, Scott wheeled around and started to flail. His body was jerking as if he'd been hit by ten thousand volts of electricity.

"Are you okay?" I shouted over the music.

"What do you mean?" Scott asked, waving his arms wildly. And that was when I realized that Scott was . . .

. . . well, he was *dancing.*

There's just no nice way to say this: The guy was doing a "Frantic Fish Flapping for Air" impersonation.

Fiona and Lucia were standing at the edge of the dance floor. Lucia looked like she was watching a horror movie — and Fiona looked like she was about to star in one. Like she might freak out and go all Freddy Krueger on Scott for dancing like an ostrich on fire. I felt half the eyes on the dance floor gaping in our direction. A hot flash of embarrassment shot through me.

"What's wrong?" Scott asked, pulling out a wobbly spin move. "You're not dancing." And then he smiled at me. It was that same heart-melting smile that always turned me into a gooey bowl of oatmeal.

"Nothing," I told him. I hesitated only a moment . . . and then I started to flail, too. I pulled out my best Slinky-in-an-earthquake moves, and Scott let out a whoop.

"You're *awesome!*" he shouted.

Just then, Kiwi and Mitchie bopped over. Kiwi was hopping up and down with her arms in the air. Mitchie had her own style, which mostly involved graceful arm movements and bending her knees. I'm pretty sure that we all looked pretty ridiculous.

But it didn't matter. Okay, so I wasn't in the League — but I'd beaten Fiona at her own game. Everyone at school knew my name. And I was dancing with my new friends and the cutest boy ever.

Can anything get more fabulous than that?

Don't miss Amy's next adventure
at Allington Academy:

ACCIDENTALLY Famous

BY Lisa Papademetriou
Another
Candy Apple book . . .
just for you.